I ESCAPED AMAZON RIVER PIRATES

ELLIE CROWE
SCOTT PETERS

I Escaped Amazon Rainforest Pirates (I Escaped Book Four)

Library of Congress Control Number: 2020901697

ISBN: 978-1-951019-10-5 (Hardcover)

ISBN: 978-1-951019-09-9 (Paperback)

Cover design by Susan Wyshynski

Best Day Books For Young Readers

Caracas

VENEZUELA

Georgetown

GUYANA

ATLANTIC
OCEAN

Bogotá

COLOMBIA

Quito

ECUADOR

Macapá

AMAZON RIVER

Belém

Manaus

IQUITOS

Pucallpa

Rio Branco

Porto
Velho

Lima

Cusco

PERU

La Paz

Cochabamba

Santa Cruz

Brasília

BRAZIL

BOLIVIA

Rio de
Janeiro

São Paulo

PACIFIC
OCEAN

MAP OF
SOUTH
AMERICA
&
THE AMAZON
RIVER

CHAPTER ONE

November 2017
Peru, South America
The Amazon River
10:00 PM

The shouts woke Nick.

He bolted upright in his bunk, his forehead stopping mere inches from the ferry cabin's low ceiling.

From out on the mighty Amazon river came men's cries. Angry. Loud. Yelling orders in thick, accented voices. He peered out the window and spotted at least four speedboats buzzing the ferry like flies.

Adrenaline fizzed through his veins. Jumping down, he opened the cabin door a crack. The narrow passageway was dark and deserted. He glanced at Madison. His eight-year-old stepsister was fast asleep. Typical.

Slipping out, he locked her in and ran down the shadowy corridor. Nick leaped over a room-service tray stacked high with dirty dishes. He eased open the deck's swinging doors and peered out.

His stomach dropped. He had to steady himself, and not because the boat was rocking.

On the ill-lit deck, passengers lay with their hands and ankles bound. A woman he'd seen snapping pictures that after-noon sobbed. Her husband looked stunned. By the bar, the dark-skinned bartender knelt with his wrists tied behind his back. Three massive hooligans, their faces painted in black-and-green camouflage, loomed over him.

Pirates!

Nick had warned his stepdad about modern-day pirates weeks ago. He'd read that they were attacking boats on the Amazon. He'd tried to show Aiden the news articles. His stepdad had ignored him.

Now, thirty feet away, the tallest pirate waved a lethal-looking rifle. Others in military-style jungle-uniforms yelled orders at cowering passengers. With jabs and thrusts of flashing knives, the outlaws pillaged wallets and valuables.

Nick's mind focused on one thing—making sure his mom wasn't out there. He scanned left and right, relieved to see no sign of her.

Then he spotted the friend he'd made earlier, a guy around his age. Tey knelt on the edge of the group. Nick groaned. But he had to get back to the cabin, he had to find his mom.

As he raced away, gunshots shattered the night. His heart hammered triple-time. This was crazy.

He found Madison sitting up in her bunk. Mom wasn't there.

"What's happening?" Madison sobbed, way too loud. "Where's my daddy?"

"Shhh!" Nick warned, his head spinning.

Madison screamed, "I want Daddy!"

"Quiet," Nick warned again.

Still howling, the stupid kid leaped up and bolted for the door. Nick grabbed her and clamped his hand over her mouth. Madison bit him. Hard.

Nick held on tighter. "Shhh!"

Madison kicked and thrashed.

"Be quiet!" he whisper-shouted. "Madison! Do you want to get us killed?"

The super-brat chomped down even harder and then screamed, "Daddy!"

If the pirates heard, they'd be here in seconds.

Where was his mom? Where was Aiden when they actually needed him? Nick had to get help. And to take care of Madison, whether she wanted him to or not.

What was he supposed to do now?

CHAPTER TWO

Eight Hours Earlier
Iquitos Port, Peru, South America
Early Afternoon

*N*ick sat along the ferry-boat railing, scrolling through his Instagram feed. At least he had Wi-Fi, even though it was spotty.

Their big boat was still moored to the shore. Below his dangling feet, the Amazon river's coffee-colored water surged past. Vendors bobbed alongside in dugout canoes. *"Cigarrillos, cigarillos! Mangos!"* they shouted. *"Pollo Asado señores, Pollo Asado."*

It was hot. Muggy. Sweating crew members hauled food crates and diesel oil drums across rickety planks. They deposited them in the bottom deck's hold. Already the top and middle decks were jam-packed with people and luggage.

Passengers who couldn't afford cabins laid claim to brightly-colored outdoor hammocks. Kids raced around screaming, babies cried, and crated chickens cheeped.

Nick's buddies back home were all jealous that he was on a year-long road trip and missing school. Secretly, though, he missed California. He missed hanging out and surfing blue waves, laughing and joking around. Not that he'd ever admit it, they'd think he was lame!

He clicked open the Santa Monica Beach surf cam. *Excellent conditions, offshore winds, shoulder-high-to-overhead waves.* He groaned out loud.

"Hey! That your surfboard in the cargo hold?" The voice had a strong local-sounding accent.

Nick looked up to see a dark-skinned teen around his age with wiry black hair knotted behind his head. The guy eyed the surf cam on Nick's phone. He looked like one of the Amazonian Indians they'd seen in the villages between Lima and Iquitos. The guy carried a fishing line and was attaching a piece of chicken skin to the hook.

"Yeah, the board's mine." Nick's blue-and-white Liquid Sword surfboard was his pride and joy. He'd insisted on lugging it along, but hadn't had much chance to use it.

The guy tossed the baited line into the river. "Where you going to surf?"

Was he joking with him? No—he looked serious. Nick shrugged. "I surfed in Lima. At Mira Flores. And in Baja."

"Wow." He looked impressed. "You on the road for a long time?"

Nick made a face. "You can say that again."

"That your family campervan in the hold? California license plates?"

"Yep."

This guy sure was observant. Either that or they didn't get many campervans around here.

"You have big surf in California, hey?" he asked.

They sure did. Surf and sunny beaches. Skateboarders zooming around smooth concrete bowls. Coca Cola, cheeseburgers, pizza . . . what Nick wouldn't do for a big, juicy slice of pepperoni pizza.

He grinned, shrugged, and said, "You got it."

"How far you go?"

"To Manaus, Brazil."

"Whoa." The guy's brows shot up. "Long way."

"What about you?" Nick asked, curious.

"Not far. I visit friends."

"By yourself?" Nick glanced to the bar where Aiden, his stepdad, was guzzling beer. "Cool."

The guy laughed. "That your dad?"

"Stepdad," Nick corrected him. He'd been living in close contact with Aiden in the small campervan for the last ten months. What he needed was a break from it all.

"Got one!" shouted the triumphant local and tossed a wiggling fish onto the deck at Nick's feet.

Nick reached down.

"Whoa! Don't touch!" the guy yelled. "It bite your fingers off!"

Nick pulled back fast. Flopping across the deck, the mean-looking fish snapped its knife-like teeth. Two local kids shrieked and scrambled up onto a chicken crate.

"Is piranha." He grinned. "Eat meat. Even human flesh." Grabbing his net, he scooped up the fish.

"Do people really get eaten by piranha? I mean that you know about?"

The guy snickered. "Yeah, they eat dead *bandido*. Lots of those around." He tossed the fish into his bucket. "We cook these tonight, you and me. Piranha taste good. Taste like meat.

You'll see."

Nick scratched his ear doubtfully. "Uh, okay?" Then he found himself grinning. In the last ten months, he hadn't met many kids who spoke English. Not since his life had radically changed. Not since Aiden had decided to haul them all on a South American odyssey in a beat-up campervan.

It was Aiden's dream, and it had become his mom's dream too. Nobody checked what Nick's dream was. He couldn't believe he'd had to miss the school trip of a lifetime to Bali with the Santa Monica High surf team.

He'd tried to win over his mom by saying, "But I'll be missing a whole year of class!"

Aiden had rolled his eyes.

"We'll be world-schooling you," his mom beamed. She'd given him a stack of home-school assignments on Mexico, Panama, Columbia, Peru, and Brazil. All the countries they'd be visiting.

Parts of the long journey had actually been fun. Parts, he had to admit, had been amazing. But he wanted to go home. To sleep in his own bed, in his own bedroom. And not in some tiny campervan with his mom, Aiden, and his bratty stepsister, Madison. Nick had only known Aiden and Madison for a couple of years, and he still felt like he hardly knew them—or even wanted to. He missed his buddies like crazy.

At least he could make a South American friend here.

"I'm Nick," he said, sticking out his hand.

"Tey." The kid took it, and they shook. When he grinned, he showed three missing teeth.

"Did you learn English in school?" Nick asked, impressed at how well he spoke.

"A little," Tey said. "I learned on the river. I work sometimes on the boats and passengers, they speak English. You come to see the pink dolphins?"

"Yeah." Mom and Madison really wanted to see pink dolphins. "You know where they are?"

Tey shook his head. "No more. Amazon Indians ate them."

Nick gaped at him in surprise. "Ate them! Ate pink dolphins? There are seriously no pink dolphins left?"

"Not many. Not many monkeys left either. All eaten. Amazon people are hungry."

Nick turned and studied the bustling river port of Iquitos as the crew finished loading up. Guys and girls roared around on motorbikes. Others partied in waterfront cafes. They all looked fine. They were having a better time than he was.

"People in Iquitos seem to be doing okay," he said. "Those are some expensive motorbikes."

Tey laughed. *"Bandido,"* he said. *"Bandido* make big money on the Amazon."

CHAPTER THREE

Iquitos Port
The Amazon River
Late Afternoon

*L*ate sunshine blazed through the cabin windows. Water slapped and rowdy chatter drifted up from the crowded port. In the distance, thick clouds hung over the jungle. Onboard, everything and everyone smelled sweaty and dank.

"You stink," Madison told Nick.

He pretended he hadn't heard her, but knew she was right. He grabbed the towel housekeeping had left on his bunk, along with a change of clothes. A short way along the corridor, he found a door marked Baño/Bathroom.

But when he opened it, he stared and muttered, "Weird."

The shower head was right over the toilet. Should he stand on the seat? Straddle it? How were you supposed to shower?

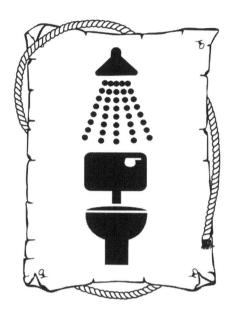

He hung his towel where he hoped it wouldn't get wet. Then, with one leg on either side of the toilet seat, he turned on the faucet. A few sluggish brown drops hit his head. And stopped. He thumped the showerhead. Nothing.

"Bummer!" At least he hadn't soaped up. He pulled on his North Face T-shirt and khaki shorts. His stomach rumbled. He'd told Tey he'd find him later near the top-deck bar. They sold cokes and chips that would hold him over until dinner.

Suddenly, the ship's engine clanked and rumbled to life. The boat was on its way at last.

He swung by their cabin, found it empty, chucked his dirty clothes and towel inside, and headed for the deck.

His mom spotted him and called, "Nick!" Blue eyes shining, she beckoned him over. "Beautiful, isn't it?" She pointed across the wide river to the emerald-green jungle. "We'll be seeing a lot of that in the next few days."

"Yeah. Amazing," he said.

Waves rocked the barge as they chugged away from shore.

"Hungry?" his mom asked. "Aiden's getting Madison. Oh, there they are. Aiden!"

Nick's stepdad and stepsister weaved unsteadily through the crowd, grabbing onto benches to keep balance. Once the four of them claimed a table, Mom and Aiden went to grab food.

Madison kicked her feet and ignored him. Nick looked around.

As the red sun sank into the water, the river barge was coming to life. Sunbaked men played cards, arguing fiercely and then roaring with laughter. A mustached guitar player strolled around, strumming a lilting ballad. It clashed with the thumping Latin pop music coming from the bar. Nick's new friend, Tey, was nowhere in sight.

"Here we are," Mom said, handing Nick a bowl of fried chicken strips and warm tortillas.

"Thanks, Mom." He wrapped a piece of chicken in a tortilla and took a big bite. The chicken was good—tough but spicy. Nick grabbed two more chicken strips before Madison got her hands on them. For a skinny kid, Madison ate a lot and she ate it fast. He'd learned to grab his share when she and her six-foot-tall dad had joined his family.

"People sure know how to enjoy themselves here," his mom told Aiden, giving him a hug. "I love it!"

Madison shot Nick a look, and for once, they both seemed to be thinking the same thing. Would Aiden and Mom ever want to stop traveling?

Would they ever get to go home again?

CHAPTER FOUR

Ferry Boat
The Amazon River
9:00 PM

Sweating in the dark, stuffy cabin, Nick listened to the creaking barge. He'd left Mom and Aiden swinging in a hammock on the top deck. He'd wanted to stay and enjoy the cool air and fun scene but had been sent down to babysit. Talk about unfair. How had Madison become his responsibility? They weren't even related. Well, not by blood.

At least she was asleep. With her glow-in-the-dark blond hair, she looked harmless. But he knew better. The kid snoozing in the bottom bunk was trouble.

Madison was still steaming mad that her dad had married Nick's mom. Well, Nick didn't like it either. He and his mom had been fine after his parents' divorce until Aiden came along.

Mom said Aiden was fun, with his free, wandering lifestyle as a photo-journalist. She claimed he was 'exactly what they needed'. But Nick didn't want a stepdad. He was still sore at his own dad for taking off. And he sure didn't want a stepsister.

He could hear faint rock music. Sounded like fun. He longed to be on deck. Rolling over, he pulled the pillow over his head.

He was almost asleep when someone thumped on their door.

"Nick? Nick? Are you awake?" The voice came in a loud whisper.

Nick sat up, squinted. Climbed out of his bunk and opened the door. "Tey?" he said. "Wassup?"

"Nothing. Uh—is okay if I hide my stuff in your camper-van, Nick? Is that cool?"

"Why?"

"For tonight. I get in the morning."

"What kind of stuff?"

"Just—my things. Nick—I need a safe place, okay?"

Tey seemed weirdly stressed, but Nick saw no reason to say no. Tey was probably freaked out about sleeping with his wallet on deck or something. "Sure, I guess it's okay. But it's locked."

"I put through small window at back. Okay?"

"Oh," Nick said. How did Tey know the window at the back of the campervan was funky? Well, no one could climb through that small window anyway. "Yeah. No problem. See you tomorrow."

"*Gracias,*" Tey said. Like a shadow, he disappeared.

Nick bolted the cabin door. Now that he thought about it, Tey had looked terrified. Something else seemed weird: there were no engine sounds. The ferry had stopped. Maybe the captain dropped anchor at night?

He climbed back into his bunk, yawned, and dozed off.

CHAPTER FIVE

Ferry Boat
The Amazon River
10:00 PM

The shouts woke Nick.

From the dark river came men's cries. Loud. Angry. Yelling orders in thick, accented voices. He peered out the window and spotted at least four speedboats buzzing the ferry like flies.

Adrenaline fizzed through his veins. He hustled from the cabin and ran down the long passageway. As he stared out the swinging doors, Nick's stomach dropped. He had to steady himself, and not because the boat was rocking.

On the ill-lit deck, passengers lay with their hands and ankles bound. A woman he'd seen snapping pictures that afternoon sobbed. Her husband looked stunned. By the bar, the dark-skinned bartender knelt with his wrists tied behind his back. Three massive hooligans, their faces painted in black-and-green camouflage, loomed over him.

Pirates!

Pirates had taken over the ship.

Nick scanned left and right, searching for his mom. He saw no sign of her and breathed out, relieved. Then he spotted Tey kneeling on the deck's far side. His jaw tightened. So this is why Tey wanted to hide his stuff in the campervan; he knew pirates were coming!

And Tey hadn't even bothered to warn him.

Nick felt beyond stupid for trusting the guy. Here he thought he'd made a friend. Yeah, right.

He had to get back to the cabin. As he raced away, a gunshot shattered the night. He ran faster.

Moments later, he came panting through the door.

"What's happening? Where's my daddy?" Madison sobbed.

'Shhh!" Nick warned, his head spinning.

"I want Daddy!" Madison screamed, bolting for the door.

Nick grabbed her and muffled her mouth.

Madison bit him. Hard.

Nick held on tighter. "Shhh!" he hissed. "Madison! Quiet!"

If the pirates heard, they'd come looking. Men, armed to the teeth. She'd get them killed. He felt sick knowing Mom was out there—and Aiden, too.

He spun Madison and crouched, his face inches from hers. "Listen to me. Your dad's coming. Okay?" he lied. "So quit shouting like an idiot."

He couldn't believe it actually worked. She wiped her nose and glared at him.

Nick needed to think. He needed to send out a call for

help. Did Peru have a 911 emergency number? He grabbed his iPhone. No service.

But Wi-Fi was spotty, it might come back online.

Thumbs flying, he text-messaged his grandpa in Los Angeles, California.

911! We're on ferry boat Fortuna. Sailed today from Iquitos. Pirates on board. Guns. Can't find Mom. Call U.S. Embassy. Help!

He prayed the message would get through. Grandpa was a war vet, he'd know who to call . . . If he got the message.

Madison climbed under the covers, eyes peeled wide, and whispered, "Where's my daddy?"

"He'll be here."

Nick knew what would happen next. The pirates would start searching the cabins for more people to rob.

He started grabbing their valuables: his iPhone, Mom's tablet, Aiden's laptop and cameras. He shoved them under a mattress. Not a great place, but they were out of sight. At least their passports, cash, and credit cards were locked away in the campervan.

"What are you doing?" Madison whispered as he changed into a black long-sleeved shirt.

"Nothing." There was no time to explain that he hoped to stay invisible while he searched for their parents.

Outside, something banged into the boat below their window. He risked a peek out of the porthole.

Way below, two of the large speedboats had been roped onto the lower cargo-hold rails. They bobbed in the water. In them, stood five huge men armed with assault rifles. Their silhouettes loomed against the ink-black sky.

Was this for real? They looked like the bad guys in *Borderlands 2*.

One pirate barked orders into a VHF radio. Another

scanned the river with what looked like high-powered binoculars. The rest started rigging up a pulley system.

Madison tiptoed up. Together they watched the pirates swing suitcases, crates and drums onto the speedboats. They were stealing them from the cargo hold! This was insane. Armed pirates had taken over and they looked scary professional.

Nick crept to the door and checked the bolt was locked.

He had no clue what to do. He only hoped his mom and Aiden were holed up somewhere safe.

CHAPTER SIX

Ferry Boat
The Amazon River
10:05 PM

*N*ick took up a position against the door, pressing his ear to the battered wood. Outside, voices echoed down the hallway. This was it. They were coming. Nick's grip tightened around Aiden's heavy, three-legged camera tripod. It was the only weapon he could find.

Madison huddled next to him, shaking. "Are the pirates coming?"

"Shhh."

"Will they steal our stuff?" Madison hissed.

"I hid everything. Stay quiet."

"What about the stuff in our campervan?" Madison whispered in his ear. "You told that guy he could hide his stuff in there. You said it. I heard you."

She'd been awake that whole time?

"Yep, I did," Nick said.

"Daddy's gonna be mad. You're going to be in trouble. He has to ask Daddy, not you."

Nick flicked her away from his ear. Madison was an annoying know-it-all, and she was right. He should never have told Tey it was okay.

Footsteps hurried along the outer metal passage. Someone was coming. Madison stared at him, wide-eyed. Then she dove for her bunk and pulled her blanket over her head. Tripod in hand, Nick pressed against the wall.

The knob rattled. A key scraped the lock. His mom and Aiden charged inside, looking pale and shattered.

Madison threw herself at her dad, sobbing.

"Mom!" Nick said, holding on tight as she pulled him in for a hug. "Are you okay?"

"Yes." She was panting. "They didn't see us. We were in the hammocks on the top deck."

"Is anyone hurt?" he asked.

She glanced quickly to where Aiden was comforting Madison and whispered. "I'm not sure."

The sound of a gunshot shattered the air and everyone flinched.

Aiden pulled out his iPhone. "Still no Wi-Fi."

"What are we going to do?" Nick's mom asked.

"I don't know, but we're the only Americans on board," Aiden said. "If they find us, they're going to hold us for ransom."

"Oh god," Nick's mom gasped. "We have to hide."

"Where?" Aiden asked.

Nick's mom began straightening the sheets. Aiden gaped at her, but Nick caught on and started helping

"Hurry," she said. "We have to make the cabin look empty. Quick! Make up the bunks. Nick and Madison, you two hide underneath. Creep under as far as you can, pull your backpacks in. Daddy and I will go down the hall and hide in the bathroom."

"No!" Madison clung to Aiden. "I'm staying with Daddy."

"Okay, okay," Aiden said. "I'll hide with Madison. Sarah, you get under the other bunk with Nick. Drape the blankets so they hang down."

They moved frantically, getting to the floor.

Nick's mom crawled in first and he crowded in next to her. After a moment, she whispered, "Aiden, what about our stuff in the campervan? Our passports? Our cash? Did you lock the safe?"

"Of course I—"

But Madison cut Aiden off. "Nick's weirdo friend hid something in our camper," she announced. "Nick said it was okay."

Nick cringed. What a tattletale!

"What friend?" Aiden demanded, his voice low and outraged. "What did he hide?"

Nick cleared his throat. "His name's Tey. And he's not a weirdo," he said, although he now feared Tey was no friend. "It was just his phone and wallet."

"You sure?" Aiden asked.

"Yeah, what else would he want to hide?"

"I don't trust any of them," Aiden muttered. "I hope he hasn't found our passports and cash. How would he get into the campervan?"

"He didn't. He shoved them through the rear window." But

Nick no longer felt certain. What if Tey had broken in? He felt angry and guilty all at once. "I'm grabbing our stuff from the safe."

"No!" his mom said. "Stay put!"

But before Aiden and his mom could stop him, Nick got up, snatched the campervan's keys, and ran out the door.

CHAPTER SEVEN

Ferry Boat
The Amazon River
10:15 PM

*N*ick raced along the passage on tiptoe, pausing to listen every few moments. He reached the metal ladder leading to the cargo hold and clambered down. Every muscle fired with adrenaline.

The place overflowed with cars, pick-up trucks, motor-bikes, and bicycles. Crates, drums, and bulky dark shapes loomed under eerie orange lights. He scanned the gloom. Were pirates somewhere in the shadows? Hard to say.

Better get moving. He crept down a cramped aisle and froze. The scrape of heavy objects being dragged toward the waiting speedboats echoed loudly.

It was too late to turn around. Taut with tension, he

reached the campervan, unlocked the door, and climbed inside. For a moment, he sat there catching his breath. No one came to investigate.

In the back, Tey's stuff lay on the bunk where it had slipped down from the rear window. It was a lot more than a wallet and phone. Nick picked up a long hard object wrapped in a garbage bag. What the heck? He unrolled it and found himself holding a weapon he'd only seen in video games and on TV.

A rifle. A big, black assault rifle.

Why would Tey own an assault rifle?

The van made a soft creak. Nick's eyes snapped up and his heart slammed off-kilter.

"What is it?" came a demanding whisper.

Aiden. He'd followed him.

"A rifle," Nick said.

"Sheesh. And your friend put it in our campervan? Let me see that thing."

Nick handed it over, biting back a warning when Aiden turned on his flashlight app. Was he crazy? At least he shielded the light with his hand.

"An AK47?" Aiden said hotly. "Why would some kid have an AK47? What else is in there?"

Nick pulled out a beat-up leather jacket, a phone, and a square box made of dried, woven palm leaves. It was bigger than his outstretched hand.

Aiden took it, unwound the string closure, and opened the lid.

Together they bent close to stare at half-a-dozen lumps of dried clay. Aiden moved the light closer. The chunks shimmered with soft, yellow gleams.

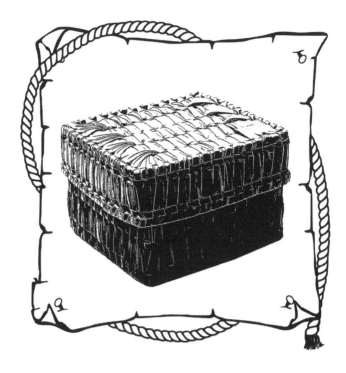

"Gold!" Aiden breathed. "It's raw gold!"

"What, seriously?"

"Careful, it's gold amalgam, the flakes are mixed with mercury," Aiden said. "It's poisonous to touch."

Nick stared at the crazy hoard. He glanced up into the darkness and then back at what they'd found. Tey had raw gold? No wonder he wanted to hide it. So that's why he had a gun. What the heck was Tey into?

The ferry boat rocked hard, letting out a long moaning sound.

Voices echoed on the far side of the cargo hold. His stepdad clicked off the phone's light. Motioning Nick to be quiet—as if he needed the warning—Aiden raided the storage bin for supplies. He pulled out two mosquito nets, two hammocks, the water filter, and insect repellent. Then he unlocked the safe and grabbed the passports and cash. Quickly, he stuffed the documents and supplies into his backpack.

Motioning Nick to follow, he climbed out of the camper-van, taking Tey's stuff with him.

"What you doing?" Nick whispered.

"I'm not having that rifle and gold in my campervan." Aiden set Tey's possession alongside some plastic crates. "If the police arrive and find that stuff in my vehicle I'll be arrested."

Nick had to admit it was a smart move.

Still, as Nick followed his stepdad back to the cabin, his skin crawled. How would Tey react if the pirates stole his rifle and gold? No doubt he'd be furious.

Nick didn't much like the threat of having Tey as an enemy.

That could be dangerous.

CHAPTER EIGHT

The Amazon River
10:25 PM

$\mathcal{I}$n the cabin, Nick and Aiden crammed into their hiding places.

Then, his mom and Aiden started to argue in furious whispers. Aiden had this crazed idea that they should abandon ship. He'd become frantic.

"It's too dangerous here. We're Americans. They'll hold us for ransom. They'll kill us. They're pirates. Life is cheap to them. I don't trust the crew either. That Tey kid had raw gold. Illegally mined, I'm sure. And an AK47."

Nick's mom sounded ready to cry. "We can't just go out on the Amazon River. We're in the middle of nowhere!"

Right? Come on! Jump into that massive, brown, fast-flowing river? And what—swim half-a-mile to shore? With the caiman and piranha, and who knew what else? Nick agreed with his mom. What right did Aiden have to order them around? Nick's dad would never do this. He'd said this whole South American trip was crazy. Nick should've gone to live with his dad. And no way did Mom want to jump ship!

"It's the Amazon River!" she whispered, sounding hysterical. "What lunatic would take his family out there? There're anaconda, Aiden! Forty-foot snakes! And piranha. Plus electric eels. Massive caiman. This is a huge river, one of the biggest in the world. You want us to swim to shore? That's insane."

"We've got the surfboard." Aiden's voice was flat. "Nick can hold Madison on the surfboard and we'll kick alongside. We're only about a mile, two miles max, to shore."

Two miles?

His mom said, "And if we make it? Then what?"

"You saw the huts and villages we passed. We'll find someone with a car or truck. Even motorbikes. We'll pay them to take us to the airport. We have cash and our passports. It's all we need."

"It's too dangerous," his mother said.

Suddenly the cargo boat shuddered. The engines thumped into action.

"We're moving again," Aiden said. "The pirates are taking the boat to shore, Sarah! They'll find us. We're sitting ducks. We have to go. While we still can."

She pushed Nick out from under the bunk and crawled out after him. She wore a wide-eyed, trapped expression. "Nick. Madison. Put on long-sleeved shirts. And jeans. Bring ponchos. Aiden, where are the passports? Put them in Nick's backpack. Hurry."

"Can I bring my new Lego dollhouse?" Madison said.

"No." Aiden snapped. "Get dressed, Madison. Fast." Face

grim, he wrapped his cameras, their phones, the passports, and cash in a waterproof bag. He shoved it into Nick's backpack. "Got to be life vests on this piece of junk," he muttered, glancing around.

Nick looked at his mom. Surely she'd stop this crazy plan?

"The vests are here," she said, breathless as she pulled them from a cabinet. "Put them on. They fasten in front. With that clip. Hurry."

Faces mutinous, Nick and Madison struggled into life vests as Nick's mom and Aiden did the same.

"Okay. We move fast and silent," Aiden said. "Remember the pirates are on deck, so no talking. We go to the hold, grab the surfboard, and jump off."

Aiden sped them toward the campervan.

"Hurry!" Aiden hissed.

For a nerve-wracking moment, Nick couldn't find his backpack. Turned out Madison was sitting on it. He grabbed it and tied it to the base of the surfboard leash.

On the bottom level, a sluggish breeze wafted over the railing. Nick's mom paused, holding on and staring down at the Amazon River. Her lips moved in prayer.

Rowdy voices echoed from the far end. Nick's heart pounded.

Together, Aiden and Nick pulled the surfboard off the roof.

The ferry boat chugged along. Dark-brown water rippled in the moonlight. Aiden wrested control of Nick's surfboard, set it on the surface, and slipped in after it. Holding the board's leash, he reached up with his free hand. "Sarah, lower Madison down. Nick, climb on behind her."

They were really doing this?

This was the most insane thing Nick could ever imagine. With no other option, he climbed over the railing and dropped into the river. The water felt warm. Madison clung to the front of his board. He hoisted himself up behind her and inhaled the familiar smell of surf wax. His Liquid Sword! He'd relied on it so many times. It felt reassuring.

A surge hit, and Madison yelped. The kid didn't want to do this anymore than he did, he thought with a flash of sympathy. It would be even scarier for her. She'd only just learned to swim. He patted her leg as they bobbed up and down.

Madison kicked him. Hard. Right on his nose.

Right, he thought. Last time I try to help that brat.

The cargo boat loomed over them, looking massive. This was so weird. Way scarier than paddling out in huge surf. To his left, he could see the pirates' speedboats. With a chill, he eyed the jaguar heads painted on the prow of the biggest motorboat. The sooner they got away the better. At any moment, the pirates could spot them.

With a splash, his mom was beside the surfboard, spluttering, her face tense.

"Mom, get on," Nick said. "I'll swim." He didn't even want to think about what could be in the water. Anaconda, alligators, caiman, electric eels, piranha. You name it, the Amazon River had it.

"No, I'm fine," his mom said. "Hold on to your sister."

No way, Nick thought, I'm not holding that brat. Not unless I want another kick. And she's not my real sister, anyway.

"Let's go!" Aiden said. "See those lights? That's an Indian village. We're going there." He kicked off from the cargo boat and gave the surfboard a hard push.

Around him, waves rippled and crested. They were moving toward the far shore—the opposite direction of the cargo boat. The current moved with them. That was good. It would help them get there. But the small lights of the Amazon Indian village seemed miles away.

Nick heard his mom and Aiden splashing to keep up.

"Mom!" Nick called.

"I'm fine," his mom gasped. "Keep hold of Madison."

Nick knew his mom was a strong swimmer. Still, the life vest hampered her stroke.

His dad would never have taken his family out here. Why had his parents gotten divorced? Aiden was a maniac. Maybe after this, his mom would go back to his dad. He hoped so.

"Keep moving!" Aiden said. "Paddle!"

His mom and Aiden swam, and Nick paddled hard. It was challenging with Madison on the front. An eddy took them and sent them bucking sideways over small waves, riding high over the ripples.

Madison screamed.

"You're not gonna fall off," Nick told her.

Glancing back at his mom, he tried not to think about piranha with their sharp pointed teeth. Piranha that hunted in packs and stripped flesh from bones in seconds. He couldn't believe she'd gone along with this! If she got hurt, he'd be furious. She should be on the board, not him!

"Mom, get on here, please?"

"No, I'm fine, keep going."

Wasn't there something about a creepy toothpick fish? Yeah, that's right. Did Aiden know about that tiny monster? If only he'd mentioned it earlier. Aiden might not have been so keen to get into the river. The toothpick fish loved the smell of urine. That's why it swam up a man's urethra and stayed there. He shuddered.

"Don't pee," he warned Madison.

"You're weird," Madison hissed. "Poopyhead."

He laughed in spite of himself, he was losing it. Madison shot him a grudging grin. Nick rolled his eyes and laughed again.

"Keep going!" Aiden panted. "Nick, paddle!"

"I'm paddling!" he said.

In minutes, the boat's dark outline faded into the distance. The lights from the coastal village disappeared too. The family was alone in a world of inky-blackness on the mighty Amazon River.

"Keep moving," Aiden gasped. "We're doing good."

Nick looked back. He couldn't see his mother. "Mom!" He squinted. "Where's mom? Mom!"

"Sarah!" Aiden turned. "Sarah, are you okay?"

It all happened fast.

The surfboard took off. A wave grabbed hold and sent it careering forward. One moment, the family was together. The next, Nick and Madison were on their own, caught in a current, tossed by a whirlpool, hanging on for their lives.

Desperately, Nick tried to turn the board around. The

current was too strong. Again and again, he screamed for his mom.

Madison's voice rang out in a panic-stricken shriek. "Daddy!"

She struggled to her knees, rocking the surfboard.

"Get down, Madison," Nick yelled. "Lie still! You'll fall off!"

"I want Daddy!"

The surfboard tilted.

Aiden's voice carried in the wind, words lost in the tumbling water.

It sounded like it was coming from a long way off.

CHAPTER NINE

The Amazon River
10:45 PM

*N*ick snatched Madison from the current. She sobbed as he hauled her on board. If the river had swept her away—well, she couldn't swim to save her life.

He was desperate to turn back for his mom, but Madison made that impossible.

The second they reached the shore, he'd drop her off and go back. Alone, he could paddle like a demon.

Tossed by waves, struck by spray, Nick paddled hard.

"Hold on tight, Madison! We'll make it."

His stepsister had gone strangely silent.

A black wall of jungle appeared, towering above the river. Land. Finally.

"Madison," he said. "Watch for the village!"

A right-hand bend was coming up. If he kept the surfboard straight, the current would suck them to the bank. He saw no lights anywhere. Had they swept past the village?

"Rocks!" Madison screamed.

Nick back-paddled furiously. Too late. With an ominous thump, the surfboard hit a jagged boulder head-on.

Madison flew head over heels into the water.

Nick tumbled off, and his feet touched mud. He caught hold of Madison and helped her onto a jutting rock.

"Stand here," he said.

Luckily the surfboard hadn't snapped in two. Here, in the shallows, the river churned up mud, and branches swirled. Giant logs—felled, abandoned trees, he realized—knocked and rolled against one another. He looked for the best way to get Madison to shore.

A splash made him whirl around. Oh no! His stepsister had jumped off the boulder. With grim determination, she charged toward shore through the knee-deep water.

"Wait! Get back here!" Nick shouted.

He saw it before she did. The whirling water was alive with silver fish. Thrashing fish. A feeding frenzy. Piranhas chew flesh down to the bone with their razor-sharp teeth. They strip a body in minutes.

"Madison!" he shouted. "Get out of the water!"

"Something bit me!" Madison shrieked. "Something bit me!"

Abandoning the surfboard and the attached backpack, Nick thrashed through the churning water. His every nerve cringed, waiting for, expecting, the sharp bite of the terrifying fish.

In front of Madison, blocking her path, was a big, thick log. Grabbing his stepsister, he was about to lift her onto the log when he took another look. The log moved. And blinked. He reeled back in horror.

The log had scales. Black, shiny, armor-like scales. This wasn't a log. This was a caiman. Bigger than any alligator he'd seen in the zoo.

Thrashing piranha leaped into the air. Jaws snapping, the caiman jumped after them. Almost hyperventilating, Nick hauled the shrieking Madison out of the water. He dodged around boulders and splashed onto the riverbank.

"Stop screaming!" he hissed. "Stop! Madison! We're in the jungle. There are dangerous animals here. They'll hear you. Let me see your leg."

Madison covered her mouth with her hand. Hiccupping loudly, she held out her leg. Dark blood covered the knee of her denims.

Nick rolled up the jeans. Her skin had only been scratched, but it looked a deep scratch. He splashed the bite with river water. How toxic was a piranha bite? Probably pretty toxic. He squeezed the scratch to get out some blood and possible poison. Madison screeched.

"Sorry! Sorry!" he said. "I'll get the antibiotic for it."

"An alligator bit me," Madison sobbed. "He tried to eat me."

"He was eating piranha," Nick said. "You're lucky he didn't eat you. You're lucky the piranha didn't eat you too. I told you to stay on the rock."

Madison gulped. Wide-eyed, she looked back at the roiling water. In the moonlight, it looked like some black and white horror flick. Nick watched the caiman's huge thrashing tail and the jumping, silvery piranha.

"He bit right through my jeans," Madison wailed.

"The caiman didn't bite you. You'd be dead. The piranha teeth scratched you."

"The caiman did. And you're being mean," Madison said. "I hate you. Wormhead!"

Nick shrugged, furious with Madison. His mom was out there on the dark river. And it was totally obvious he couldn't he leave Madison on shore. She'd do something crazy. He pressed his fists into his eyes.

His mom was a surfer, she'd taught him to surf. He told himself she'd be fine. She knew her way around in the water. Still, the thought of her out there made him sick.

He scanned for her, left and right. The water shone metallic in the moonlight. Luminous. The trees along the bank formed a dense, dark wall. Mom was nowhere in sight.

If they'd made it across, how would they find each other in this crazy jungle? He had an idea. He'd use the flashlight to try and signal them. Maybe they'd see it. Maybe they'd call out.

"I've got to get my surfboard and the backpack," he said. "Stay here."

"Noooo!" Madison wailed.

"You don't want to come with me, do you?"

Madison shuddered. "No."

"Okay. We need the surfboard and the stuff in the back-pack. Stay here. And do as I say this time, Madison. Do not move. I'll be quick."

As fast as possible, Nick made his way over the slippery rocks. He found the surfboard and backpack wedged between two boulders. After strapping on the pack, he grabbed his board. It felt great to have it under his arm. He felt better, more himself.

Again he scanned the river and the shoreline. Black water. Black jungle. Giant trees towered, their crowns disappearing in the tangle of branches overhead. Palms, some like enormous fans and others tall and slender, were covered by rope-like vines. No sign of Mom. No one except Madison, a small figure standing desolately on the bank.

She ran to meet him. "I'm freezing," she whispered.

"Me too. Hold on." He pulled a plastic rain poncho from the backpack and passed it to her. She yanked it over her head.

Nick dug out the flashlight and stood at the water's edge. Flashing repeatedly, he listened for his mom or Aiden's calls.

Deep in the jungle, something roared.

Madison jumped. "What's that?"

"I don't know." The roar sounded horribly like the roar he imagined a jaguar would make. A jaguar on the prowl. Hunting.

Something amongst the trees shrieked. A raw sound of utter terror.

ELLIE CROWE & SCOTT PETERS

Madison cried, "What was that?"

"Jungle animals," he whispered. "Jaguars, panthers, wild boars, snakes. They hunt at night. We have to be quiet."

He stared into the buzzing, honking, hooting, twittering, roaring, shrieking darkness. To those beasts, he and Madison were fresh meat. Juicy, fresh prey.

And there was no safe place for prey in the jungle.

CHAPTER TEN

The Amazon Jungle
11:05 PM

*J*agged lightning slashed the sky. Far off, thunder rumbled.

"Great," Nick muttered. "A storm's coming."

Madison hunched deeper in her poncho.

They picked their way along the shore, hopefully heading toward the village. But they needed to find shelter. Nick peered into the black jungle. There, deep in the trees, tiny lights flickered. Lots of lights. Dancing lights.

"Look!" he said, his heart leaping. "There must be people in there."

He pictured thatched huts with flickering fires.

"People?" Madison squinted. She shook her head. "No, it's

fireflies. I saw fireflies at the zoo with Daddy. I wish Daddy was here."

She was right. They trudged on.

After a time, they came to a massive, fallen hardwood tree. Its uprooted, gnarled roots had created a small cave. It would have to do. One after the other, he and Madison crawled under the roots. Once inside the hole, they pulled the surfboard in after them. Nick blocked the entrance with broken branches and ropelike vines.

Crouched on the surfboard, he dug out a dry T-shirt and changed while Madison peeled off her rain poncho. She'd stayed dry underneath.

The bulky backpack was like a treasure chest. Inside were two mosquito nets, insect spray, antibiotic cream, aspirin, energy bars, trail mix, four water bottles, and a hand-crank-powered flashlight. There was a lot more stuff at the bottom. No wonder it weighed a ton.

"Good packing, guys," Nick murmured, thinking of his mom and Aiden. Fear rose sour in his mouth. Had they reached shore? If so, where were they? He'd go out at dawn and start looking.

Working as a team, they tented a mosquito net over their heads. Each covered themselves with insect spray. Then they wolfed down a Kit Kat bar and a handful of trail mix each and shared a bottle of water.

"Don't backwash," Nick warned.

"I already did," Madison replied.

"Gremlin."

She smirked, stuck one skinny arm in the backpack, and pulled out a fluffy pink dolphin. "Flipsea, there you are!"

"Mom packed that?" Nick said in disbelief.

Madison shook her head. "I packed her," she said defiantly.

Nick rolled his eyes.

He cleaned Madison's piranha bite and covered it with ointment. "Listen to me, Madison," he said. "If I tell you not to go somewhere, don't. You're lucky you weren't eaten by piranhas."

Madison stuck out her tongue. "Jerkface! You're not the boss of me!"

From outside, someone shouted, "Ho! Ho!"

The shout was loud. Like some strange Amazonian Santa Claus.

To Nick's horror, Madison scrambled to her feet and shouted, "Hola!"

"Shhh! Nick hissed. "We don't know who it is."

"Ho! Ho!"

"It's people!" Madison hissed back.

Together they scrambled to peek out of the shelter. There was no one in sight.

"Ho! Ho!"

"Monkeys!" Madison pointed at the branches above. "Howler monkeys! Look!"

They'd both been wanting to see howler monkeys the whole trip. This wasn't how Nick imagined it. Still, after exchanging a curious glance, they crawled outside.

In the branches above, there sat a troop of howler monkeys, black silhouettes against the canopy.

"Ho! Ho!" the monkeys hooted.

Noticing Nick, the largest monkey thumped his chest. Nick thumped his chest back. Howler monkeys! How cool was that?

"Ho!" Madison called. "Ho!"

Like acrobats, the monkeys swung from branch to branch and disappeared.

Nick slapped at the hovering mosquitoes. "Back into the shelter."

Madison shook her head. "I need to pee."

"Pee by that palm tree." Nick slapped more mosquitoes. "Hurry."

"Someone could see me."

"No one can see you."

"The monkeys can."

"The monkeys don't care."

"Don't look." Madison ran behind a palm tree. "I need toilet paper," she called.

"Good luck with that."

"You're mean."

Nick was about to pee in the river when he thought again of the toothpick fish, the candiru. Small but evil, that's how the Amazonian Indians described it. The story went that in 1997 a young man stood peeing in the Amazon River. A candiru leaped from the water and swam up his urine stream. The man tried to grab the fish, but it was too fast and slippery. It disappeared right up his urethra. The nearest hospital was in Manaus, a hundred miles away. By the time he got there, the poor guy couldn't pee, and his bladder was swollen to the size of a beach ball. At least the Manaus doctor was able to remove the candiru. But Nick was nowhere near Manaus.

He decided to pee near a palm tree instead. Better safe than sorry. While peeing, he still felt nervous—long scratches marked the palm's trunk. Some huge animal had been sharpening its claws. The jungle gave him the creeps

Above, a branch shook, and then a hard object bonked his head. Nick yelped. Another missile struck his shoulder. He looked up. A white-faced capuchin monkey sat in the palm tree, ghostly in the moonlight.

With a scrawny black arm, it picked another fruit, took a bite, and threw the rest at Nick.

Nick's stomach rumbled. Fruit! If the monkey was eating it, the fruit must be alright. He caught the next oval-shaped fruit. He guessed it must be a date and took a bite. The yellow fruit tasted sweet.

"I want one!" Madison tasted the date and licked her lips. "Look, he's little, he's only a baby."

The monkey threw another date. Then he caught a branch with his long tail and swung away.

The wind had risen. It wailed through the jungle, shaking the trees. Rain splattered from the canopy of branches above.

Nick and Madison dived back into the shelter and pulled the fronds across the opening.

CHAPTER ELEVEN

The Amazon Jungle
Night, Day 1

*M*adison wiped her face. "It's raining in here, too."

Nick grimaced. She was right, this wasn't much of a shelter. He'd have to go back out and cut some palm fronds to improve the roof. Searching the pack for Aiden's Swiss knife, his hand bumped a square box. Trail mix? He hoped so. He pulled it out, and his stomach flipped. Tey's box of gold amalgam! What the heck? How did that get in there?

"What did you find?" Madison asked.

"Nothing." He shoved the palm-leaf box to the bottom. Yikes. He thought Aiden had left Tey's stuff in the ferry's parking bay. Clearly not.

Uneasily, Nick wondered how much the gold was worth. A

thousand dollars? Ten thousand? More? Tey must be freaking out. Had he stolen it? Were its owners hunting it down? Would Tey tell them Nick took it?

Nick pictured a gang of fierce Amazonian Indians and felt sick.

Should he ditch the gold? No, if he ran into Tey, that would be worse. He'd have to hold onto it.

People would be searching for it. People with guns—most likely Amazon gold pirates. And somehow that freaked him out even more than the wild beasts hidden in the jungle. His family had escaped the boat, but they were in more danger than ever. What had Aiden been thinking?

A rain splatter landed on his head. "Wait in here," he told Madison. "I need to fix the shelter."

The night was wild and getting wilder. With wind and rain lashing, he hacked at fronds. One by one, he draped them over their cave, anchoring them with rocks, overlapping them to form layers.

Not bad, he thought, surveying his handiwork with the flashlight.

In the darkness behind a fan palm, something shifted in the shadows.

Something—or someone—was watching.

He went still. Cold filled him. There it was again. A figure was stalking him.

Was it a howler monkey? They were big. Big enough to be dangerous.

No, monkeys didn't stalk. Monkeys weren't predators.

He dived head-first back into the shelter.

Inside, he switched off the light. Wrapped in the poncho and the mosquito nets, he perched on the hard surfboard. Madison curled up next to him and tried to get comfortable.

"This is not a good bed," Madison whined.

"Shhh," he whispered. His ears positively twitched, listening to the night.

Within minutes, Madison was snoring.

Easy for her, but no way could Nick sleep. He checked his iPhone. Still no service. He wished it would ring.

Last year, when they still lived in a nice solid house, Madison had hidden his iPhone. She'd found a good spot too—in a box of crackers at the back of a kitchen cupboard. Then she'd gone to her room and kept texting and calling it. He'd run around for half an hour searching for it before clueing in to the fact he was being pranked. Of course, Aiden had argued that she was a little kid, and Nick was old enough not to get mad.

He got her back later, though. When she was asleep, he poured warm water on her mattress. *Ha!* It was great payback, too. Her red face told him she was sure she'd wet the bed. To make it even better, he'd kept whispering what Aiden had said, *she's a little kid*, whenever he passed her.

Despite his hard work outside, rain still dripped through the palm fronds. He moved closer to Madison and pulled the poncho over their heads. She felt hot. He was responsible for the little troublemaker now. Already, Madison had been almost killed by piranha and a caiman. And they'd only just got here! How long could they survive alone?

He'd read the *SAS Survival Handbook* cover-to-cover multiple times. He knew that even the smallest cut could turn septic in the wild. The second Madison woke up, he'd reapply ointment to her scrapes and change the dressing.

Something else worried him. How did Tey's box of gold get into the backpack? Why had Aiden put it there? Had he been protecting it or stealing it? Aiden was a jerk. But surely he wasn't a thief. That gold was worth a lot. Tey had to know it was missing by now. Did he think Nick had stolen it? Yeah. Of course he did. Nick tried not to picture Tey's huge gun.

Something roared. He jumped.

Was that a jaguar?

Was a giant cat on the prowl, sniffing around their cave, its yellow eyes gleaming? He knew all about jaguars, the Amazon's dominant predator. More than he wanted to at the moment. Native Americans called them *yajuar*—he who kills with one leap. Some Indian tribes call them *eater of souls*. Jaguars caught their prey by the head and crushed their victim's skulls in their powerful jaws. But Nick couldn't help wondering if they played with their victims first, the way housecats do. He'd once saved a bird from his neighbor's sadistic cat. The memory made him shudder.

The feral roar came again.

Closer now. Was that a sniffing sound? Could the jaguar smell them? Of course it could. He had to do something, this was an apex predator. They'd never escape it. Jaguars run faster than humans. Jaguars climbed trees. They could swim. They could claw their way into this cave. Indeed, the branches began to move.

Nick had to attack first. He'd only get one shot.

He rummaged in the backpack for Aiden's lighter and the insect spray.

"What are you doing?" Madison whispered.

Nick held his fingers to his lips.

He crawled forward and peeked out.

The jaguar was there!

Like a nightmare come true, he saw it through the tangle of roots and palm fronds. A massive, black, cat. The glow of yellow eyes. A real live fricking jaguar was right outside their shelter, looking in.

With an unnerving flash, he remembered the scratches on the tree. Jaguars claw-marked their territory. He and Madison were sheltering under the jaguar's tree. Maybe even inside its cave!

Boom, boom, boom, his heart throbbed in his ears.

He raised the insect spray can. I hope, I really, really hope this works, he thought. He pushed the spray button, and at the same time, he lit the lighter.

With a thrill of success, he saw flames flare along the stream of insect spray. The jaguar reared back. It disappeared into the jungle.

Madison looked at him, open-mouthed. "Wow!"

"I know!" Nick grinned. "I can't believe that worked! Wow!"

They huddled together, both speechless. There was no sound of the jaguar.

I looked right into the eyes of a real, live jaguar! he thought. I bet few people have ever done that!

The roar of the Amazon River was as good as a white noise app. Nick closed his eyes. He didn't have a clue what to do next. Things are always better in the morning, he told himself. His mom always said that.

But he knew it wasn't necessarily true.

CHAPTER TWELVE

The Amazon Jungle
Dawn, Day 2

*C*rash!

What the heck was that?

Torrential rain battered the shelter's fragile roof. Cold rain showered Nick's forehead and rolled down his neck. Everything was sopping wet.

Another ear-splitting crash exploded. The earth shuddered.

Madison screamed.

Another crash. And another.

What was going on? An earthquake? Sounded like a war.

"There's water under me," Madison yelped, jumping to her feet. "Lots of water."

Nick sat up. She was right, his butt was in a pool of water.

He pulled aside the fronds to look out. Crash! A giant tree thundered to the ground before their shelter.

"The trees!" Madison cried. "The trees are falling down!"

Nick sprang to his feet. Horrified, he watched a massive hardwood tree uproot and take two trees with it. They were right in the middle of the action. Their shelter, he realized, was the result of a tree uprooted in a previous storm.

"Hurry!" he said, "The river's flooding its banks, it's turning the ground to mud. That's why the trees are falling. Grab your stuff." They'd have to abandon the surfboard. It would be faster to run. He secured it to a root, hoping they could come back for it, and shouted, "We have to get out of here."

Strapping on the backpack, he urged her outside.

Together, they stepped into a hazy white world of rain and fog. Rain pelted down, drops so hard they stung his arms. Fallen trees lay on top of one another, leaving gaping craters where they'd been uprooted. Water swirled around Nick's ankles. The sandy bank had disappeared and the Amazon River, a raging body of fast-flowing mud, surged past. It tossed around trees, branches, and logs in wild abandon.

Gasping, water to her knees, Madison clung to her pink dolphin.

Nick grabbed her hand. Her fingers were like icicles. "We've got to get to higher ground. Hold the branches. Pull yourself along."

Mud dragged Nick down, squelched in his shoes. It was hard, really hard to move and pull Madison. She was waist-deep now, her small face white, her blue eyes huge. She slipped, pulling Nick down with her.

"My dolphin!" she screamed. "Flipsea!"

The pink dolphin sailed off, bobbing in the muddy water.

For a ghastly moment, Nick saw Madison's head go under. A surge propelled them into a bamboo thicket. Flipsea was impaled on a sliver of bamboo. With a sob, Madison grabbed her.

Before Nick knew what was happening, the ground swallowed him. One moment, he was standing in water and mud; the next, he was sinking.

Down he went. Fast. Up to his hips. The mud was thick and gooey. Quicksand! This had to be quicksand. He'd always imagined quicksand would be one of the worst things in the world. It was.

"Nick!" Madison shrieked. She lunged toward him.

"No!" he yelled. "Don't come here."

Frantically, he tried to pull up his legs. His knees wouldn't move. He was trapped and the heavy backpack was sending him deeper. He tried to get it off, but every move sent him deeper. He was sucked to his thighs. To his waist. Don't struggle, he warned himself. Struggling makes it worse. Oh god, how do I get outta here?

"Nick!" Madison cried, tears and rain streaming down her cheeks. "You're sinking!"

Swim, he told himself. You're supposed to try and swim. He'd seen it on a survivor show. Would it work? He leaned forward over the mud and moved his arms as if swimming. Concentrating, he fluttered his legs in a crawl swimmer's kick.

Slowly, slowly he inched forward. It was working. It was really working!

He reached the bamboo. Madison forced a thick stalk down over the quicksand and Nick grabbed it. Grunting, he pulled his way to firmer ground.

He was out—covered in mud, but out.

"Thanks, Maddy," he said. "You helped a lot."

Madison threw her arms around his waist and hugged him. "You nearly sank," she sobbed. "Oh Nick, you nearly sank."

"We have to get out of this water," he said, hugging her back. "We have to go higher."

CHAPTER THIRTEEN

An Illegal Gold Mine
Late Morning, Day 2

Always forward, never back, Nick told himself. *Always forward, never back.* He repeated the mantra over and over.

They'd survived so far. Still, Tey would be tracking them, desperate to get his gold. And the pirates were out there, too. He couldn't risk getting captured and held for ransom. Or worse, found with the gold in his pack. Had his mom even made it to shore?

Would they all die out here?

Mom had to be alive. He'd sense if something awful had happened to her. Wouldn't he? She had to be looking for him. They'd find each other. They'd escape this horrible nightmare.

Always forward, never back. Nick kept walking.

Madison broke into his thoughts. "I only hugged you 'cause I was scared I'd get left by myself."

"I know."

"You're not my real brother," she said.

"And you're not my real sister."

She shot him a flinty look.

"Can we keep going?" he said.

On and on, they trudged through the dripping green. No sign of people. No sign of animals. After what seemed like hours, they came to a forested bank. Slipping and sliding, they grabbed hold of branches and pulled their way up.

Atop the slope, the rainforest abruptly ended. A vast muddy field stretched before them. It was gorged with stumps, big holes, and sad-looking fallen trees.

"Someone cut all the trees," Madison said. "The rainforest is gone."

Nick couldn't believe his eyes. A chunk the size of ten football fields had been torn away. The green, beautiful rainforest had morphed into a post-apocalyptic, end-of-the-world landscape.

Without the protection of trees, rain lashed from all sides. In the distance, Nick spotted a blue tarp. It had to be a makeshift camp. He scanned the area. Deserted.

He pointed. "Let's go there."

This place had to be an illegal gold mine. Maybe where Tey dug up his gold.

Nick and Madison splashed past mounds of crushed rock and dirt. Craters oozed pools of toxic-neon yellow water, and mining equipment littered the ground. Excavators, a gas-powered pump, metal poles, sieves, cables, black hoses, and lethal-looking animal traps.

A sickly, yellow-green stream ran past carrying dead, rotting fish and birds.

"Ugh!" Madison cried. "This place stinks."

The camp consisted of a blue tarp supported by metal poles. They dashed into the shelter, pulled off their wet ponchos, and shook the water from their hair. Garbage covered the puddled ground. Empty beer and food cans and cigarette papers floated around their feet. Nick was glad to see four hammocks hanging from the cross poles, at least they could get above the water. A raised stone firepit held the charred remains of a fire.

"Why are the fish and birds all dead?" Madison asked.

"I think they ate mercury," Nick said, picturing Tey's lumps of gold amalgam. In the campervan, Aiden had warned him not to touch them. "This place is a gold mine, and the miners use mercury to extract the gold. It's poisonous."

Aiden and his mom had talked about the illegal gold mining, but he'd had no idea how bad it was. The miners had cut down the trees and poisoned the river. This was a bad scene. Uneasily, he thought of Tey's gold in his backpack. What was he going to do with it? He scanned the trees for signs of guards and saw no one.

"Who did this?" Madison said.

"I don't know."

"What about the pirates? Did the pirates do it?"

Nick wiped mud off his forehead. "I bet where there's gold, there're pirates," he said. "If we hear anyone coming, we have to hide fast. Okay, Maddy?"

Madison nodded.

"We should be okay in the storm," Nick said, for what choice did they have? "They can't mine in this mess, I doubt any miners will come out here now. We'll stay until it stops. Then we'll keep going until we reach a village."

Madison shivered.

"Look, there's some dried wood and paper under this tarp. Let's make a fire," he said.

Together, they filled the fire pit. Nick flicked the lighter and blew on the paper. Finally, it caught. With her hands warming over the flickering flames, Madison gave a shaky smile. He smiled back.

Together, they hung their clothes to dry. Wrapping up in the ponchos and mosquito nets, they curled up on hammocks. They guzzled water and ate two peanut-butter protein bars each.

Madison looked longingly at the remaining protein bars. "I'm still starving."

"Me too," Nick said. "But we better save some."

They'd been walking for hours, and this had been their only food. What would they do when the bars were gone?

"Let's take a nap," he said. "At least we won't have to think about eating."

Exhausted, he fell asleep immediately. He dreamed the school cafeteria was serving pizza—great big slices of spicy pepperoni and sausage and juicy pineapple. The whole class was wolfing down pizza and calling for seconds. The principal said they'd get pizza every day. He and his friends all cheered.

He woke feeling happy. Pale, afternoon sunlight streaked the misty sky. In the far distance, beyond the shelter, he spotted a menacing column of thick, rising smoke. The rainforest was burning! Was that a different illegal mining camp? Or farmers clear-cutting land with no regard for the rainforest?

Uneasily, he watched the distant sky grow dark with fire-flecked clouds. He pictured ancient hardwoods burning and animals fleeing.

This place was full of danger. The sooner they escaped the better. He wanted to go home.

He turned to see if Madison was awake.

The brat's hammock was empty.

CHAPTER FOURTEEN

The Amazon Jungle
Late Afternoon, Day 2

With his backpack thumping, Nick raced across the mud. In the hazy half-light, the gold mine looked like the dark side of the moon. He saw no sign of his stepsister.

"Madison! he shouted. "Madison!"

Why the heck would she take off? How could she act so crazy? She was only eight and he was fifteen, so it was up to him to take care of her. But how could he keep her safe when she kept doing stupid things?

"Madison!" he shouted. "Madison!"

He spotted a trail hacked out by the gold miners that led into the hazy jungle. Pulse roaring in his ears, he peered into the thick green rainforest. Anything could be hiding in the undergrowth.

Something could have already eaten his stepsister. He hurried onto the path. Soon, strange wild jungle sounds surrounded him.

Ho! Ho! hooted a howler monkey.

Tonk-tonk-tonk! called a flock of white birds.

Cri-cri-cri pi-pi-yo! screamed a small gray bird.

In the undergrowth, cicadas screeched.

He dreaded hearing a jaguar's roar or a panther's growl.

"Madison!" he shouted again. "Maddy!"

Then he saw her.

Madison, looking completely relaxed, sat next to the trail on some crushed ferns. In her lap, she held the small capuchin monkey.

"Look, Nick," she said beaming. "Isn't he so cute?"

Nick felt hot with anger. What a dumb kid! "Madison, what are you doing?" he shouted. "Are you crazy? I can't believe you just took off!"

Madison pouted. "The little monkey came to visit me," she said. "Then he ran away. So I followed him. He's so sweet. He's tame. See, he has a collar."

Nick looked closer and saw that the monkey had a collar made of woven palm leaves. He had to be someone's pet. Relief flooded him.

"Put him on the ground," he said. "Maybe he'll go back to his village."

"Okay!" Madison beamed again. She set the little monkey down. "Go home, baby, go home."

The monkey scampered along the trail.

"Follow him!" Nick said.

Together, they ran after it.

This trail must lead to an Indian village, he thought. I bet our parents are there!

He was desperate to see them. To know they were safe.

The monkey skidded to a stop. It whooped. A blood-chilling whoop. A warning.

Madison grabbed Nick's arm "What's wrong with it?"

The monkey was screeching at something in the bushes.

Then Nick saw it, a monster half blended in the shadows.

A giant, green anaconda.

Head raised, tongue flicking, the snake fixed its eyes on the monkey. Nick's blood ran cold. Time stood still. A scene from *Predator* raced through his head.

Lightning fast, the gargantuan snake uncoiled and pounced. It wrapped itself around the monkey. Once, twice. The monkey disappeared beneath the muscled scales.

Madison screamed and ran to help.

"No!" Nick grabbed her hoodie and pulled her back.

"It's going to kill him!" she screamed. "It's going to squash him!"

That massive snake could eat all three of them. Crush them to death. First the monkey, then Madison, then Nick. It could swallow them in turn and throw them up to make room for another. Save all three bodies to eat at its leisure.

In seconds, all Nick could see of the monkey was its little furry feet. The gleaming coils tightened. The anaconda was squeezing the monkey to death.

"Make it stop!" Madison begged. "Nick! Make it stop!"

Nick ran forward. Staying well away from the snake's head, he tried to uncoil the thick, muscled beast. He couldn't. The snake only tightened its grip. Twenty feet of undulating coils. There was no way he could unwind the monster.

The monkey had stopped struggling. The anaconda was killing it before their eyes. Nick thought, frantically. Surfers knew what to do in a shark attack. Strike the gills. Jab your fingers in the shark's eyes. Would it work with an anaconda? Only one way to find out.

Standing behind the anaconda, he gripped its head and jammed his thumbs into the snake's eyes. With a shout, he pushed with all his strength.

The anaconda reacted immediately. It reared back. As its coils loosened, Nick grabbed the limp monkey and pulled hard.

He retreated up the trail shouting, "Run!" Fast. Puffing. Triumphant.

"You saved him!" Madison screamed, sprinting alongside him. "You saved him!"

When they finally paused for breath, she stroked the monkey and murmured, "It's okay now, baby. You're safe, baby."

The monkey stirred and opened its big, round eyes.

An Indian girl came hurtling down the trail, braided hair flying. "You find!" she shouted. "You find *Hermano Mono!*"

"We saved him from a big snake," Madison said.

"You save him? *Gracias!*" The girl claimed the monkey from Nick's arms and began petting him. *"Gracias!"*

"Hola!" Nick said grinning. "It was nothing."

All at once, everything was better. Here was someone who clearly wasn't a pirate. The Indian girl must come from the village they'd seen from the river. She wore a frayed, brightly-patterned skirt and a mud-stained, orange T-shirt. Leopard-like spots had been inked along her arms. On her cheekbones, black triangles were etched in rows. White feathers shone in her ebony braids. Standing as tall as Nick, she studied him with dark, slanting eyes.

"Where you come from?" she asked. "Where you go?"

Nick struggled to remember some Spanish but couldn't think of another word. "We're lost."

The girl shook her head and looked puzzled.

Nick pointed at the monkey. "Your monkey?"

"Si." The girl smiled shyly. *"Hermano Mono.* Brother monkey"

"Oh!" Madison cried. "I wish I had a monkey."

"Si!" the girl said. "Why you here?"

"We are lost. We need help," Nick replied. "Can you take us to your village?"

"Help?" The girl nodded. "I take to mission school?"

They had a mission school? What a relief! There'd be English-speaking missionaries. Maybe even Wi-Fi. He could contact his parents or the US Embassy.

"Yes!" Nick said. "Great. Is it nearby?"

"No. Is far. First, we go village."

"Okay." Nick nodded to show his agreement.

CHAPTER FIFTEEN

Amazon Rainforest Village
Late Afternoon, Day 2

The girl led them down the sandy trail. Madison ran along, laughing at the monkey as it swung from tree to tree. Nick followed close behind.

"What's your name?" Madison asked the girl.

"Ronin Biri," the girl said proudly. "Means Shining Anaconda."

Madison looked sideways at Nick and then said. "Oh! Um, cool name! My name is Maddy."

At a bend in the trail, they heard loud voices. Five tough-looking Amazon Indians appeared—men in mud-stained clothing carrying hard hats and machetes. Their eyes narrowed at the sight of Madison and Nick.

"Hey *gringo*," called a bearded man, who carried a long-bladed knife. "What you doing in the jungle?"

Ronin Biri rattled off some words Nick couldn't understand. He sensed her fear, though.

The bearded man eyed Nick and Madison in a way that made his hair stand on end.

Ronin Biri spoke again, more urgently. Finally, the man shrugged and laughed, showing a mouthful of blackened teeth. She motioned Nick to keep walking. Nick felt relieved when the five guys disappeared down the trail.

"Gold miners." Ronin Biri said. *"Mal hombre."*

Nick wondered how she'd gotten rid of them. He waited for her to say more, but she stayed silent.

"Gracias," he said.

Ronin Biri shook her head and made a noise that sounded a bird's wailing cry. The sound was chilling. Nick realized that she was warning her village of their arrival. A moment later, they reached a grove of banana and papaya trees and small vegetable gardens.

Madison dug her elbow into Nick's side and whispered. "Look at that!"

A dark-skinned man stood in the shadows watching them. He wore a huge, live anaconda draped around his neck!

What the heck! Was that the same anaconda?

"Don't stare," Nick muttered, taking Madison's hand. "Look friendly."

A scrawny dog crossed the field, barking, and then followed them with its tail between its legs.

Next came four giggling children, holding out their hands. "Bubblegum! Bubblegum!" they shouted.

"No gum!" Madison said.

The children pointed at Madison and shrieked with laughter.

She shrugged, looking confused.

The village consisted of a cluster of wooden huts with palm-thatched roofs. Tall hardwoods circled the huts, and the ground sloped toward the rushing river.

In front of the first hut, a woman sat weaving a basket. She stared at Nick and Madison. A little girl, wearing no clothes, ran up and touched Madison's hair and then ran off, giggling.

"They're all being mean about my hair!" Madison said.

"It's different," Nick said.

"Yeah, right."

A squat man with a bowl-cut hairstyle emerged from a hut and stared stone-faced at them.

"*Hola!*" Nick called.

No response.

"They don't like us," Madison whispered.

Another man emerged from a hut. This one was tall and thin with a ballpoint pen pierced through his right earlobe and a bow and arrow in his hands. He joined the onlookers, unsmiling.

Nick felt a quiver of unease. The villagers didn't exactly seem friendly. And if Mom was here, she'd have shown up by now.

His heart sank. He'd been sure he'd find her in the closest village.

Ronin Biri led them to where a woman sat stirring a bubbling pot of stew. It smelled great.

Nick's stomach rumbled. He smiled at the woman. *"Hola!"*

The woman, whose round cheeks were covered with black wavy lines, frowned and muttered. "Awww!"

At least she looked sympathetic. Self-consciously, Nick wiped mud off his face. She nodded at him in a sort of friendly approval.

He turned to Ronin Biri. "Can you ask if anyone has seen my mom? *Mi Madre?*" He wished he'd paid more attention in Spanish class. Though he didn't know if the villagers were even speaking Spanish.

"Madre?" Ronin Biri shook her head.

Clearly, the girl had no clue what he was talking about. She spoke rapidly to the woman who looked puzzled and shook her head, too.

"Eat?" Ronin Biri asked.

"Yes! *Si!*" Nick and Madison replied together.

A little girl with black geometric shapes across her cheeks handed them each a small bowl of stew. It tasted good, some sort of potato-like vegetable with small pieces of chicken.

"Thank you," Nick said. *"Gracias."*

"De nada." The girl blushed and grinned.

De nada—Nick was pretty sure that meant, it's nothing. But three more children had lined up for food, and the pot wasn't that big. It was generous of Ronin Biri and the woman to share. He wished he had something to offer in return. When he got back to Iquitos, he'd send Ronin Biri a gift via the mission school.

The smoke from the fire drove away the hovering mosquitoes. He pulled off the heavy backpack and sat down on a woven mat, stretching out his muddy legs. It was so good to eat at last. He slurped the stew.

"Good?" Ronin Biri asked, smiling.

"*Si!* Your family?"

Ronin Biri nodded. "Auntie. Isa Rabi."

"What does her name mean?" Madison asked.

"Means Proud Bird."

"Nice!" Madison reached out and touched Isa Rabi's long necklace of nuts and white feathers. "Pretty," she said.

Isa Rabi smiled.

A familiar voice rang out. "Hey, *gringo*. What you doing in the jungle? You trying to die?"

CHAPTER SIXTEEN

Amazon Rainforest Village
Late Afternoon, Day 2

*N*ick stared in surprise. *Tey!*
He jumped to his feet.

Tey wore a red bandana around his forehead, low-riding khaki shorts, and no shirt. His massive gun was slung across his back. A black snake tattoo covered his right arm, the snake's head wrapping around his shoulder. He looked muscled and older than he'd seemed on the cargo boat, and a lot less friendly.

For a moment, Nick had almost been glad to see a familiar face.

But Tey's box of gold amalgam lay hidden in his backpack. How should he handle this? Mentioning it suddenly seemed like a bad idea. Tey would think he stole it.

"Hola!" Nick said. "Is this your village?"

He noticed Ronin Biri was concentrating on stroking the monkey's fur. She didn't look up, didn't greet Tey. She didn't even smile. There was some vibe going on here.

"What happened with the pirates?" Nick asked.

Tey ignored the questions. He motioned Nick to walk with him along the river.

"What you doing here?" Tey demanded, his voice gruff.

"My stepdad wanted to get away from the pirates," Nick said. "But my sister and I got lost. We're looking for our parents."

"I saw your mom and dad," Tey said.

Relief flooded Nick. They were alive! "Where are they?" he asked eagerly. "Where did you see them?

Tey pointed downriver. "At the mission." He studied Nick. "So, where's my box, Nick?

Uh oh!

This was bad! Tey had sneered when he'd said his name. Nick's heart began to thump in fear. He wanted to return the gold. But how could he explain why he had it? Tey would punish him, that much was clear. But how badly? Would he kill Nick for stealing it?

"Your box?" Nick said.

"I hid my stuff in your campervan," Tey said. "And now, my box is gone."

"Yeah?" Nick was beginning to get mad. "That's not my fault. You shouldn't have put that gun and your gold there in the first place. You had no right. My stepdad was furious."

Tey took a step closer. Nick could smell his sweat, see it glistening on his muscled forearms. "How you know I had gold in that box?"

Oh crap. Nick felt blood rising hot into his face. How stupid was he to give away what he'd seen?

"My dad opened it," he said. "He wanted to know what you'd put in our campervan."

"So your dad stole my gold?"

"No. Aiden's not a thief!" Nick's heart was thumping fast. Where the heck was this going?

Aiden must have stashed the box in Nick's backpack. But why? Would Aiden do a thing like that?

He decided to attack instead of defend. "Why did you hide it in our campervan?" he said. "Where did you get gold anyway? Gold mining in the Amazon is illegal."

Tey spat. "Illegal! This whole place belongs to my village. The gold mine too. The pirates bring in the equipment. We Indians do the work, and the miners pay us almost nothing!" He spat again. "Three dollars a day to mine the gold for them! Hard work. So we take. I take the gold to Manaus. I sell. Now you steal my gold."

"I didn't steal your gold," Nick said, hotly. "I'm not a thief!"

"You tell me where my gold is, or you very sorry, gringo." Tey flexed his hands.

Tey's hands were very big. Enormous, in fact.

Nearby, two tough-looking Indians with black snake tattoos circling their chests stood watching.

Tey flicked a glance at the Indians. "Other guys' gold too, gringo," he muttered. "You tell me quick or you end up piranha food."

"Nick!" Madison left the fire pit and ran up, dragging the backpack behind her. She pulled at his arm. "Let's go, Nick. I don't like it here."

Nick didn't like it here, either. Mind spinning, he tried to think of how to escape. This was getting worse by the moment

The roar of engines buzzed from downriver.

Five large speedboats, white water spraying, roared across the Amazon River toward them. The river police! Just in time!

By the fire, Isa Rabi dropped her bowl and screamed, "*Vamos!* Go! Go! Go!"

She grabbed two kids by their hands and bolted for the rainforest. Ronin Biri and the other children scurried after her like chickens after a mother hen.

Nick stared at the powerful, speeding boats. They were the same boats he'd seen the night of the ferry attack. Weapons bristled amongst the men aboard. Blacks scarves covered their heads, with slits for their eyes. On the leading boat's prow, a pair of painted jaguar faces leered.

Dread filled him. The pirates!

Now he understood. They owned the illegal mining camp —and these Indians were working for them. But someone had tipped off the pirates that Tey was stealing their gold. That's why they tracked Tey to the ferry! To catch the young thief. That's why they'd attacked the ferry in the first place! They knew he was on board.

And now Nick and Madison and his whole family were caught up in this mess.

Robbing and terrorizing the passengers had just been a bonus for the pirates. As would be holding Nick and Madison for ransom.

"Boats!" Madison cried. "It's my Daddy!"

Before Nick could stop her, she ran to the river shouting and waving her arms. "Daddy!"

Nick caught her with a flying tackle. "They're the pirates!" he hissed.

Two women washing clothes in the river abandoned their laundry and barreled past. He whirled around to see what the other villagers were doing, but there wasn't a single Indian in sight. Everyone had fled on swift bare feet. Within seconds, the place had emptied.

His knees shook. Adrenaline rushed through his veins.

"Where's Ronin Biri gone?" Madison cried.

Like the bird she was named after, she'd vanished into the jungle.

He hauled Madison toward the trees, risking a glance back at the pirates. Tey was talking to the guy in the jaguar-prow speedboat. He was jabbering fast, gesturing, explaining something. Then he pointed right in Nick's direction.

So that was how Tey planned to get out of this mess, huh? Throw Nick and Madison under the bus?

Assault rifles and machetes in hand, the pirates grinned at Nick—the kind of evil grins *mal hombres* give you before they cut your throat.

Nick wasn't waiting around.

Dragging Madison behind him, he charged into the jungle. They ran and ran, stumbling over and over. Leaves and branches slapped their faces, and vines tore at their legs. They didn't stop until their throats hurt, and their hearts felt like they'd explode.

Together, they stood still and listened. There were no sounds of people. No sounds of anything except birds and the drip, drip, drip of water plopping from the forest canopy high above.

They'd ditched the pirates. But now, they were totally lost.

And night was coming.

CHAPTER SEVENTEEN

Amazon Jungle
Morning, Day 3

They'd spent the night wrapped in mosquito netting, huddled under thick leaves. When dawn came, they sat up and grinned at each other, proud they'd managed to stay alive another night.

"I want to go to that mission place," Madison said, puffing as she stumbled behind Nick. "The one Ronin Biri told us about."

"Me too," Nick grunted.

There was no sign of a trail, only endless soaring trees and tangled vines. The mission was their only hope of survival, but Ronin Biri said it was far away. She'd pointed downstream, in the direction the water was flowing. If they followed the river, they'd find it.

He hoped.

Listening hard, he could make out the faint roar of the river in the distance. First, they needed to reach its shores. Then, they'd have to risk staying close to the water to avoid getting lost again. But Tey and the pirates would be on the lookout. They'd know Madison and Nick would try to get to the mission. They'd be searching along the riverbank for signs of them.

Nick felt furious with Tey. How could he betray them like that?

After the heavy rains, even more insects had appeared. Mosquitoes, flies, and gnats swarmed in clouds around his nose and eyes. The mosquitoes carried malaria and dengue fever and all sorts of jungle diseases.

"I wish Daddy and your mom were here," Madison whimpered. "I wish Ronin Biri would come back."

"Me too. Those Indians sure know how to disappear."

Yes, like jaguars and anaconda knew how to disappear, until they wanted to eat you.

Nick scanned the underbrush, towering trees and twisting vines. He saw no movement, but he knew animals were watching. Animals camouflaged by spots and stripes. Animals hiding in hollow trees, under bushes, in burrows, under roots. Animals crouching in the canopy's tangled branches above.

The Indians were invisible too. Hiding in the shadows. If you lived in a kill-or-be-killed world, a world full of enemies, being invisible was critical.

He and Madison needed to be invisible.

The jungle was a constant battle of life and death.

"Keep going," Nick said. "Let's find the river."

They wandered for hours, coming to dead ends and turning around. Finally, pushing through the undergrowth, they came upon a narrow Indian trail. They followed it, moving as quickly and silently as possible. The path zigzagged through the rain-drenched trees and soggy thickets. Half the time, Nick wasn't even sure they were on the trail.

After a while, Madison stopped and listened. "The river!" she whispered. "We're almost there."

Nick could hear the rushing water too. The river sounded like a friend.

They must have circled back to the village without realizing it, for he sighted a hut ahead. They crouched low and ran to the shelter of a clump of banana trees.

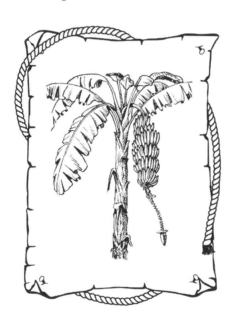

Clouds of yellow butterflies fluttered around them. Red macaws swooped overhead.

Madison grabbed a pale yellow banana, peeled it, and took a big bite. She grimaced and whispered, "Tastes funny."

Nick tried a bite. The starchy banana stuck to his tongue. "Must be a plantain. Probably have to cook them."

Madison looked ruefully at the inedible banana. "I'm starving."

"I know. Me too."

Amongst the dried banana leaves lay a nest with four small white eggs. He cracked one and sniffed the yolk. "Smells okay."

Holding his nose, he swallowed the egg raw.

"Yuck! I'm going to puke," Madison groaned.

"Eat one. It's not bad."

"No way. I'd rather starve."

"Suit yourself. Let's go."

Nick leading, they skirted around the village, staying hidden. They couldn't take any chances that the pirates or Tey might be there.

On the far side, they reached a muddy trail and trudged along the riverbank. On their left, the bank dropped steeply to the water. Every now and then, gnarled branches or collapsed sections forced them to detour into the jungle.

Madison spotted it first. She gave a delighted squeal. "Your surfboard! This is where we slept!"

He couldn't believe it. She was right!

Running forward, she peeked into their old shelter. "Can we stay in here for a little while?"

Nick shook his head. "We better keep going. It's already late. We'll use the surfboard, and we can get to the mission before dark."

"No, I'm scared to go back on the river. That's how we got lost!"

"We'll be fine. Put on your life vest. Luckily, they didn't wash away." He broke a long straight branch off one of the fallen trees. He'd use it for a pole. "Come on," he said. "Let's do it."

Surfboard under one arm, backpack strapped on his back,

Nick led the way down onto the muddy bank. At a section of boulders, he stopped and fastened the leash around Madison's wrist.

"Keep this on. Okay? Even if you fall off the surfboard, you can use the leash to pull the board back to you."

Madison gulped. "I don't want to. The water's going too fast."

She was right. The Amazon River looked wild and dangerous. But what choice did they have?

"We'll stay close to the shore."

He studied the fast-flowing river. There were riffles of white water, which he wanted to avoid at all costs. About to lower the surfboard into the water, he stopped mid-stride.

"What the heck!" he cried. The nightmare was happening all over again!

The boulder at his feet wasn't a rock. Like before, he was about to step onto a caiman. A great big caiman, fourteen-foot or more, with one beady red eye focused right on him. Had he learned nothing about this crazy place?

"Wait!" he gasped. "There're caimans all over!"

Madison shrieked.

They were surrounded. The alligator-like creatures lay still, so still, halfway underwater. Waiting. Watching for their next juicy meal.

Madison turned to bolt for shore. Nick grabbed her. The rushing river offered their only escape.

"Let go!" she yelled, wiggling furiously.

"Cool it!" With Madison under his other arm, Nick threw down the surfboard on the river's surface. He jumped on, taking her with him.

"Nooooo!" Madison wailed.

She sprawled on the front of the surfboard, and Nick gave

the board a swift, practiced shove. The rushing current swept them up. And then they were moving away. Fast.

They were clear.

Breathing heavily, Nick lay his cheek against the warm surfboard. He inhaled the sweet smell of wax. It was still there, the smell of the ocean. If only the surfboard could zap him back there. Back home.

He heard a noise, like an explosion of air. Like a big fart. What now?

"Did you fart?" he said. "Give me a break, Madison. Your butt is right by my head, you know."

"No!" Madison said, indignantly. "I didn't do anything." Then she let out a delighted squeal. "Oh! Nick, look! There's a pink dolphin."

The pink dolphin, head popping out of the water, looked

right at them with its long-nosed, friendly dolphin face. It blew out air, making another funny farting sound. Then it dived under the water and disappeared.

"I saw one! I saw one first!" Madison yelled. "I can't wait to tell your mom!"

Nick grinned when she turned to look at him, and she grinned back.

After the storm, the river was running wild. The surfboard careened through the bucking waters.

They sped along close to shore, but Nick could see jagged rocks sticking out of the water. If they hit one, the board could buckle and sink.

No sooner had he thought it than a large boulder appeared. And they were heading right for it.

Madison screamed. "We're going to hit!"

Pole out, Nick shoved at the boulder. The surfboard swerved. But the current pounding against the rock had formed a treacherous whirlpool. Caught in the whirlpool's vortex, the surfboard began to spin.

"Hold on!" Nick shouted.

Above the chaos came the roar of engines. *Please let it be a rescue boat*, he prayed. Straining his eyes, Nick tried to make out what was coming. The leading speedboat bore down on them.

On the boat's prow, he saw the twin faces of a snarling jaguar. Then he saw the thugs and their leering grins.

The pirates.

They'd been found.

The pirates began to shout, making wild, scary noises. Inwardly, Nick shook with fear. He and Madison had to get back to shore. They had to hide.

He shoved at the boulder with all his might. The whirlpool

spat them out, back into the rushing current, back on to the river. Right in front of the pirate's lead boat.

"Go to the shore!" Madison screamed.

"I can't!" Frantically, Nick jabbed the pole into the water, trying to spin them and head for the shore. No way. It continued its wild ride downriver. But now it was going backward.

Nick looked up straight into the jaguar-faced prow. The Indian's phrase for the jaguar flashed through his mind: *He who kills with one leap.*

To his utter disbelief, a gunshot rang out.

"They're shooting at us!" Madison screamed, "Nick, the pirates are shooting at us!"

CHAPTER EIGHTEEN

Amazon River
Late Afternoon, Day 3

error ripped through Nick's body.

On the surfboard, they were easy targets. In one quick movement, he grabbed Madison and pulled them both into the river.

Now they were careening after the surfboard, still clinging to the leash.

Madison gulped and spluttered as she swallowed water.

With his free arm, Nick tried to grab a fallen tree. The branch broke off in his hand. Water rushed by, blinding, choking him.

Another volley of shots rang out.

The pirates whooped.

A harsh voice called, "Got you now, little piggies. Run, run, make it fun!"

"They're going to kill us!" Madison sobbed.

The surfboard came to a sudden halt, wedged between two rocks.

Nick felt mud underfoot.

Logs, branches, and debris from the storm littered the shore, holding the pirate boats back. Nick ripped off the leash cuff. Clutching Madison's arm in one hand and the backpack in the other, he hustled for the shore. He hated leaving his board, but they had to move fast.

More gunshots rang out. They kept running.

They scrambled up the river bank and into the jungle.

"Run, little piggies!" the pirates shouted. "Run, run, make it fun! We find you!"

Nick felt sick. The pirates knew they were heading for the mission—they were making a game of this. They'd keep chasing them all the way there. Even if they reached it, they wouldn't be safe. If only he could warn his parents that they were all in danger!

He tried to assure himself that Aiden would be on high alert for the pirates. No way would old Aiden be fooled. He was the nervous type. If he heard the speedboats, he and Nick's mom would hide. Nick hoped.

"Why do they want to kill us?" Madison sobbed.

"I think they were just having fun," he lied, not wanting to tell her about the gold and that Tey had sold them both out. They'd have to keep heading for the mission and try to stay hidden.

Deeper in the rainforest, he spotted a group of vine-strangled huts. Hope filled him. Local Indians. They'd know if this was the route to the mission.

The huts were nestled under a giant kapok tree. It towered over the surrounding jungle. Way up in the spreading branches, bats soared and dived. Pink and white flowers covered the twisting roots.

Madison sniffed. "It smells like something dead."

Nick shivered. Uneasily, he noted the ghostly quiet. No children yelling or dogs barking. The place seemed deserted.

"*Hola!*" he called.

No one answered.

Madison pointed at the kapok tree's thick trunk. "That looks like a fat person's tummy!"

Nick looked at the massive dark tree. Talk about creepy. And something really did smell dead. A dead animal? Or was it the flowers? "Don't touch it."

"Why?"

"It's called a sorcerer's tree."

Madison stared wide-eyed. "How do you know?"

"I read about it."

"So, if you touch it, what does it do?"

"Supposedly, you'll make the tree-spirit mad, and he'll blow up your stomach until it bursts."

"Yech!" Madison sidestepped to avoid the huge roots and flowers. "I don't like that story. I hope the Indians here aren't mean."

Nick pushed aside the nearest hut's woven palm frond door and peered into the gloomy interior. A ray of sunlight sent cockroaches scurrying across the floor. The shiny brown beetles crawled under woven baskets, carved bowls, and a grinding stone.

The Indians seemed to have left in a hurry. The place looked abandoned.

"Why did everybody leave?" Madison asked.

"I don't know." He surveyed the hut. The Indians had abandoned so much stuff. Had they left because they were sick? Could he and Madison catch some weird tropical disease from being here?

"I don't want to go in!" Madison said. "There're cockroaches!"

"There're hammocks," Nick said. "And it's dry. It's getting dark, and we need a place to stay tonight."

The abandoned huts gave him the creeps, but by now, he knew the jungle weather routine. Within ten minutes, rain would be pouring down.

Reluctantly, Madison entered, shivering. "I'm starved."

"You're in luck." He dug out their two remaining protein bars. He ate his slowly, savoring the peanut chocolate taste.

His stomach growled. I'm not much of a hunter-gatherer, he thought. They should teach hunter-gathering at school. It would come in handy in the event of a global catastrophe.

"I'm going back for my surfboard," he said.

"Noooo!" Madison said. "I can't stay here. It's spooky. I'll come with you."

Nick sighed. "Forget it, we'll go in the morning." He'd sneak to the river while she was asleep.

Darkness fell fast. Wrapped in mosquito netting and curled up in a hammock, Nick lay listening. The jungle was putting on its nightly sound show. Creatures screeched, chatted, buzzed, and hooted.

Madison whispered: "Nick, are you asleep?"

"Nope," he said. "What about you?"

Madison giggled.

Silence.

Outside, frogs croaked. *Coqui Coqui.*

"Do you miss your real dad?" Madison's voice sounded wobbly.

"Yeah." Nick thought about his dad, his smiling eyes and deep, reassuring voice. "I wish he was here right now."

"Were you sad when he left?"

"Yes. But I see him on weekends, it's not that bad."

"You're lucky." Madison, peeked out of her mosquito netting, looking small in the big hammock. "I never see my real mom."

"Oh." Nick didn't know what to say. "Do you miss her?"

"I sort of do," Madison said. "But I was only two when she left. And now she lives far away."

"Where?"

"In Bali."

"Bali! Why's she there?"

"She said my dad was boring and she wanted to do something exciting," Madison said. "So now she lives in Bali. She says it's an island and it's beautiful and fun and far away."

Yikes. Poor Madison. No kid deserved to be treated like that. Then he thought about his stepdad and shook his head. Had Aiden become travel-obsessed to get back at his ex for calling him boring? Too bad those two hadn't stayed married and toured the world together. Then his mom wouldn't be married to Aiden.

But when he thought of Mom, he groaned. Maybe he should give the guy a break.

Funny how Aiden and Madison never talked about her mom. Is that why Madison clung to her dad? Because she was scared of losing him, too?

"It's lousy you never see her," he said. "I hope she visits soon."

Madison kicked the wall, and her hammock swayed. "I can write her about our trip," she said. "I'll tell her we're not boring, right Nick?"

"Yeah!" He laughed. A hollow-sounding laugh. "Your mom should have come on this trip. She'd have loved it."

A blood-curling shriek rang out. A predator was making a kill. After the scream, the jungle went quiet. Deathly quiet. Smaller creatures were listening. Trembling.

There was danger around him. He could feel it.

The foul smell wafted in the flapping palm frond door.

All the Amazonian Indian myths that he'd laughed about back home no longer seemed funny. In fact, they seemed downright creepy.

Like the one about the *Mapinguari*. Half-man, half-were-wolf-like creature, it had a gaping mouth in his belly. The *Mapinguari* ate the dead and the living. Some people claimed they'd seen one for real. They said he was tall with thick fur and smelled like death and garlic.

Here, anything seemed possible. Maybe the rotting village stench came from some hungry *Mapinguari* roaming the jungle. Maybe it had killed the villagers. Maybe it was outside the hut right now.

Or maybe there really was something dead in here. Decaying bodies, lying buried in the far corner.

He couldn't leave Madison alone. His surfboard had been solidly wedged between the rocks. He'd get it as soon as it was light.

It was dark, so dark.

There was no way to see a predator—animal, human, or monster.

CHAPTER NINETEEN

Amazon Rainforest
Early Morning, Day 4

Something stung Nick's arm. He slapped it. Another sting. This time on his neck.

"Bloodsuckers!" he muttered, opening his eyes.

A thin beam of sunlight pierced the thatched roof. Nick couldn't believe he'd slept soundly all night.

He had to get his surfboard.

He jumped to the dirt floor and gasped. The cockroaches had gone, but now ants swarmed the floor. Fire ants—with bites like fire! The sooner they got out of here, the better.

He shook Madison's hammock. "Pull your boots on first, and then run outside," he said. "The floor is full of ants."

She moaned sleepily, covering her eyes with her arm. "I'm not scared of ants."

"They're fire ants. They're burning my skin off."

"Oh! Okay."

Outside the hut, the jungle hooted, sang, and buzzed around them.

"Let's go find my surfboard," he said.

"No!" Madison's voice was shrill. "I don't want to go to the river. What about the pirates?"

"We'll watch for them. We'll listen for their speedboats."

But at the riverbank, Nick saw no sign of his surfboard. He groaned. His beautiful Liquid Sword. He should've come back last night to look for it. Now either the pirates had it, or it was bobbing downriver.

Keeping a lookout, he led the way along the trail. Morning sunshine gave way to a misty drizzle. By noon, wet fog blanketed the jungle. The soggy trees dripped green.

They hadn't eaten since last night.

"Are we almost there?" Madison asked.

"Not too far," Nick said. Actually, he had no clue.

What if somehow they'd gone past the mission? What if it was inland and they hadn't seen it? That would be a disaster. The next village could be miles away.

Madison caught his arm. "Look, a house! Right on the river!"

A large wooden shack, built on stilts, stood partway out in the river. Brown water rushed around the stilts that held the hut high and dry. A wooden jetty stretched across the half-submerged mangroves, linking the shack to the riverbank.

"Wait here," Nick said.

"No!" Madison's lower lip trembled.

"Stay right here. Don't move. I'll take a look first."

He ran down the jetty. The shack was solid, its walls built

with thick planks. Iron bars covered the narrow windows. A thick metal chain secured the door.

There was no sign or sound of people. The place looked deserted, like the huts they'd left earlier. Still, along the jetty were hooks to tie up boats. The metal hooks were shiny like they'd been used recently.

Nick peered through a barred window, trying to make out shapes in the gloom.

He gasped.

Uh oh!

This was some scary hideout. Then it hit him. *This was the pirates' hideout.*

Rifles, knives, and gleaming machetes were mounted everywhere. Tall metal safes filled one wall. Glossy panther skins covered two bunk beds. A desk held a computer, binoculars, and a pair of digital scales—probably for weighing gold!

In the middle of the ceiling, the red light of a camera eye blinked. He jumped out of sight. Sheesh! What if the pirates had a live-link to the camera from their boats? What if they'd seen his face peeking in the window?

He dashed back down the jetty. The sooner they got away, the better. This had to be why the nearby huts had been abandoned. The Indians must have fled the pirates who owned this shack.

On the jetty, Madison was on all fours, peering between the wooden slats. She jumped up, bubbling with excitement. "Look down there!"

Nick eyed the mudflats under the jetty. His heart leaped when he spotted his blue and white surfboard. It was in the mangroves, wedged between the scrubby bushes. His Liquid Sword!

"Oh wow!" He grinned. "My board! Let's go! And don't step on any caimans."

Madison nodded nervously. "Okay."

They slid down the bank and into the mangroves. Could the board have washed down the river? Or had the pirates placed it there to trap him? His heart began to race.

"Quick!" he said. "We've got to get outta here."

Madison climbed onto the surfboard and scanned the water, lips pressed together.

Nick pushed off and leaped on behind her. They moved through the mangroves and around the wooden pilings holding up the jetty.

"There's something in the water!" Madison's voice was shrill.

Nick felt hairs on the back of his neck rise. Those were the worst words to hear when paddling on the Amazon. "What? Where?"

Then he saw it too. A shape bobbing in the surging water. A round shape, the size of a basketball. Going up and down under the waves of rippling water. A caiman? An anaconda?

A strange moan rang out.

"What the heck?"

Madison pulled herself up. The surfboard rocked.

"Lie down!" Nick hissed.

"It's that guy!" Madison screamed. "Tey! The Indian guy. Look, Nick. Look! He's tied to the pole. He's drowning."

Paddling furiously, Nick zigzagged between the wooden pilings.

Tey's dark eyes focused on him. A red bandanna gagged his mouth, muffling his moans and sobs. Waves crashed over his head. He was on the verge of drowning. Drowning, or getting eaten by piranhas or caimans.

Nick went cold with horror. I bet the pirates did this, he thought.

Unstrapping the pack, he reached in and pulled out Aiden's Swiss knife.

"Hang on to the piling," he told Madison. "Try and keep us steady."

She grunted with effort, doing an excellent job of it.

Working as fast as he could, he sawed through the rope twined around Tey's body. Goggle-eyed, Tey watched him. With every rising surge, the poor guy's head went under. Nick could hardly imagine a worse fate. He knew the pirates were evil. But they were crueler than he'd ever imagined.

He remembered Tey laughing and saying the pirates fed *bandidos* to the piranha. He bet Tey hadn't expected to end up that way, too.

Tey was lucky they'd found him. He wouldn't last much longer.

But if the pirates returned, he and Madison would face the same horrible fate. Tied up to the pilings. Left for fish food. What a way to go!

Heart racing, he hacked at the rope.

Finally, it fell away.

Tey wrenched off his gag. Coughing and spluttering, he wrapped his arms around the wooden piling and gasped for air.

Then Nick heard it. Coming so loud, so fast. The terrifying roar of speedboats.

"The pirates!" Madison screamed. "They're coming!"

CHAPTER TWENTY

Amazon River
Mid-Morning, Day 4

The pirate boats sped closer. In the lead came the boat with the snarling jaguar prow. Three pirates stood on board, their thick bodies silhouetted against the blazing sky. One pirate whooped. A wild whoop of victory. Another roared with laughter. The cluster of speedboats tightened their formation.

Bang! Bang! The popcorn sound of bullets hitting the water.

"Get down," Nick screamed at Madison. They'd have to dive into the river again. Hide in the jungle. But how much longer could they keep this up? How long could they keep running away?

The sound of another engine came from the opposite

direction. A big white boat wheeled around the river bend, heading straight for them.

They were trapped.

He grabbed Madison and pulled her into the water.

Then, to his shock, an air horn honked, and a voice with a distinctive Australian accent spoke over a loudspeaker. "If you look to the right, in the canopy above, you'll see a family of capuchin monkeys. See their white faces? Capuchin are considered the most intelligent monkey species. They use stones to crack palm nuts. And hey—you'll love this one, mates—during mosquito season, capuchin squash millipedes and use the juice as insect repellent. How'd you like to try that?"

A burst of laughter rang out. For a moment, the happy sound shocked Nick. It seemed crazy, with the pirates' speedboats so close.

But here was a tourist boat! A river cruise!

It was their only chance. They'd have to paddle out to it. They'd be easy targets for a few minutes. But then they'd be safe. Surely the pirates wouldn't risk an attack in broad daylight?

Nick took a deep breath. "Back on the board and hold tight," he told Madison. "You too, Tey."

"Yes. Go!" Tey growled. "It's our only chance! Go!"

With Tey kicking at his side, Nick paddled furiously past the pilings and out onto the rushing river. "Help! Help!" he yelled.

The tourist boat kept chugging by. Surely, the people had seen them? Maybe they thought they were local children, playing, yelling, having fun.

The pirates' speedboats had come to a halt. There was no laughter now. The guns were tucked out of sight. Still, ever the predators, the pirates waited, poised for action.

Heart pounding, Nick pulled himself up, first in a crouch and then standing. He raised his arms high and waved in the crisscross call for help.

"Help!" he yelled. "Help! We are lost American tourists!"

He heard Tey's deep voice. "Help! *Ayuda!*"

Madison's voice, high and piercing, joined in. "Help me! Help me! Please, please help! We are lost! We are lost!"

There was a second of silence.

Then the loudspeaker crackled again. "Children on the surfboard. We hear you. We are coming in to help you. Stay on your surfboard. We are sending a launch to bring you in. I repeat, stay on your surfboard. Do not be afraid. You are safe."

Heart still racing, Nick lowered himself back onto the surfboard. Glancing left, he saw the pirates watching.

"We're saved!" Madison shouted. "We're saved!"

But were they? The tourist boat lowered a launch into the river. A crewmember in a blue and white uniform rowed to them. Another with wild Rastafarian hair leaned down, smiling, to pull them onboard.

The pirate boats remained motionless—all except one. The boat with the snarling jaguar heads circled closer. Nick's stomach tightened. Was he putting these people in danger?

The launch reached the tour boat. Nick pulled himself up the ladder.

The jaguar boat edged closer.

He had to think quickly.

The tour boat captain's face had grown wary—it was clear he sensed danger. Nick spoke to him fast. With a muttered oath, the captain nodded, grabbed the megaphone, and handed it to him.

Nick raised the megaphone and spoke loud and clear. "People in the jaguar boat! United States and local authorities are searching for us. The captain has just radioed them our location. I repeat, the authorities have been informed of our location. We no longer need your help. Again, we do not need your help."

Beside him, the captain understood and got busy radioing someone. Nick had no idea who.

In the jaguar boat, the pirate at the wheel was close enough now to meet eye-to-eye. They sized each other up. Nick refused to turn away. Madison stood right next to him. He figured she was staring just as hard, and he now knew that she had an awesomely stubborn stare.

It was the pirate who broke their gaze. He sneered, staring at his fists. Then the thug gave a sharp nod. He was acknowledging he'd been beat! He swung his sleek boat around, gunned the engine, and took off. Together, the pack of speedboats vanished up the river.

Nick breathed out. He glanced at Madison. A grin spread across her face. Then, they both whooped and high-fived and hugged and whooped again.

CHAPTER TWENTY-ONE

Amazon River Boat
Late Morning, Day 4

On the boat, excited tourists surrounded Nick, Madison, and Tey.

"Oh my! You must be those poor little lost American kids," said a woman with a broad Australian accent. "Your mom and dad are at the hospital in Iquitos. Don't worry, honey," she patted Madison's shoulder. "They're fine. They'll be so thankful to see you."

Their parents were safe! Nick dug his iPhone out of the waterproof bag. It still worked. He connected it to the tourist ship's Wi-Fi.

Finally, he had a signal.

His mom answered, her voice shaking. "Nick? Nick? Is that you?"

"Yes!" Nick could hardly speak. His eyes filled with tears. "Mom, are you okay?"

"Yes, we're fine. Where are you, darling? Is Maddy with you?"

"Mommy!" Madison grabbed the iPhone. "Mommy, I want to talk to my daddy."

Nick listened as Madison told their story. He'd have plenty of time to talk to his mom later. He was so thankful she and Aiden were alive.

On the boat, everyone was talking about them.

Nick overheard a gray-haired woman speaking to her grandson. "Why were the kids all alone?"

"Didn't you see the news, Grandma?" The teen tapped his phone and held up the screen with a photo of the family. "Pirates were robbing their ferry boat. The family thought they were going to be kidnapped or killed, so they jumped into the Amazon River. I think the kids got lost."

"Insane!" his grandmother said. "Unbelievable!"

"Awful," a red-faced man agreed. "We weren't told about pirates attacking boats. Apparently not the first time this has happened. Tourists should be warned."

The teen moved closer to Nick. "Can I get a selfie?"

Nick nodded, and he and Madison moved in and smiled for the camera.

The captain, a lean man in a crisp, white uniform, shook Nick's hand. "You're two brave kids." He tapped his temple. "That was fast-thinking back there."

"Thanks," Nick said.

"You too, son," the captain told Tey. "Well done. Great job."

Tey said nothing, only stared at the deck, avoiding Nick's eyes.

"Bet you'd all like something to eat and drink," the captain said.

"Yes!" Madison beamed. "We hardly ate for days." She scratched the bites on her muddy leg. "Daddy says they're safe in the hospital at Iquitos. He says to call him when we're at the port and someone will pick us up."

"Okay!" the captain said. "We'll be in Iquitos around eight tonight."

A tour guide, a friendly local woman in a blue and white uniform, looked them over and winced. "Let's go to a crew cabin and you can clean up those cuts and bites. And then you're just in time for our lunch buffet. Bet you like cheeseburgers and mango ice cream?" She took Madison's hand and led them along. "I read about you two. You're Nick and Madison. Isn't that right? You're famous."

Madison beamed. "We're famous?"

"Yes. The missing American children. Your parents were found yesterday, and there are lots of people searching the jungle for you. Well, you're safe now. Here we are. Go on in and wash those scratches. I'll come back and take you to the buffet. You can even have a taste of freshly caught piranha!"

Madison shuddered. "Thank you. I'll have a cheeseburger. I don't really like piranha."

Nick sat on the crew cabin bunk. The real mattress felt terrific.

Tey stood awkwardly at the door. "*Gracias*," he said. "You saved me. I thought I was dead."

"Who tied you up?" Madison asked.

Tey spoke to the floor. "Pirates."

"Why?" Nick demanded. "I thought they were your *friends*." He knew he sounded sour. And he felt sour too.

It was Tey who ratted them out. He'd almost gotten them

104

killed. He'd told the pirates about him and Madison, and he'd obviously claimed Nick stole the gold. Nick was glad Tey hadn't drowned and was happy he'd managed to save him. He still didn't trust him, though. Tey had betrayed him.

Someone knocked at the cabin door. "Got your backpack and surfboard here," the Rastafarian crewmember said. He looked at the three serious faces, and his smile faded. "Everything okay with you guys?"

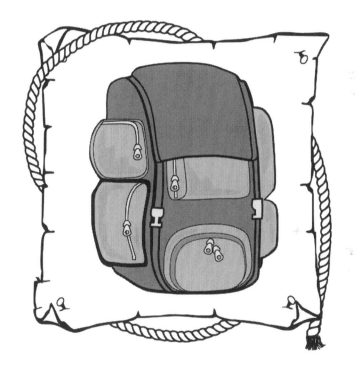

"Yes. Thank you!" Nick grabbed hold of his surfboard.

"Better get on some dry clothes and come to lunch."

Pulling off his wet shirt, Nick went to the ensuite bathroom and grabbed a towel. Tey stripped off his sopping wet shirt, too. Nick noticed Tey had a knife in his belt. A big knife. Seeing it, he wished they hadn't been left alone in this cabin together.

Madison, clueless, said, "I hope Flipsea's okay."

She put the backpack on the lower bunk and started unpacking it.

First, she pulled out her pink dolphin, stroked it, and placed it on the pillow. Then she pulled out the woven palm leaf box and laid it beside the dolphin. "Sorry, Flipsea, your bed's all wet."

Tey let out a surprised yell. He grabbed the box. "I knew it! I knew you stole it!"

Nick gulped, eyes on Tey's knife.

Like a flash, Madison grabbed back the box, clutching it to her chest. "That's mine!"

"It's not." Nick glanced at Tey, whose face was unreadable.

CHAPTER TWENTY-TWO

Amazon River Boat
Noon, Day 4

*I*n the crew cabin, Nick swallowed hard. "Madison, the box is Tey's. Give it to him."

"It's mine!" Madison wailed. "I got it for Flipsea. It's her bed."

"No, it's not, Maddy," Nick said, trying to keep the fear from his voice. "Give it to Tey."

"No! I found it on the ground. By the campervan."

Tey's eyes narrowed. "You found it by the campervan?"

"Yes," Madison said firmly. "Finders keepers. It's mine."

Here Nick had suspected Aiden when the thief had been Madison all along. She'd liked the palm leaf box, so she'd taken it, having no idea it was full of gold.

"Maddy, this is serious," Nick said. "He's not joking, hand it over."

"No." Madison shook her head stubbornly and backed toward the cabin door. "Finders keepers, losers weepers."

Tey's face was red. Any minute now, he'd lunge. Would he brandish his big knife? Nick had no wish to find out. And he didn't want Madison to find out either. He didn't want it to end this way, after everything they'd struggled through.

"Give him his filthy box, Madison," Nick said. "We nearly lost our lives because of it. And he's welcome to it. He's probably going to be killed by the pirates when they come after him to get it."

Madison stared at Nick, wide-eyed. Then she threw the box at Tey and began to sob.

Tey grabbed it. Untying the string, he lifted the lid. And then he shouted. An awful roar that made both Nick and Madison jump in fright.

"Where is my gold? *Donde diablos esta* my gold!" He flung the box across the cabin.

Nick's blood ran cold. He stared at Madison and then at the box. It was empty. Absolutely empty. Not a trace of the round balls of gold amalgam.

Tey's hand closed around his knife.

"Madison!" Nick said.

Madison reached a new level of sobs. It sounded like there was no way they would stop any time soon.

Nick shook her shoulder. "Maddy! This is very important. Listen to me. What did you do with the stuff inside the box?"

Nose streaming with snot, Madison said, "There was nothing in it. Just some mucky, yellow mud rocks."

"What did you do with them?" Nick kept his eyes on the knife in Tey's hand.

"I threw them out," Madison hiccupped. "It was just mud!"

"Where?" Tey hissed.

"By Ronin Biri's hut. Where I was playing with my dolphin."

"*Estúpida*!" Tey turned to the door.

"You're going to get it?" Nick asked.

"Si." In two strides, Tey crossed the cabin floor and took hold of Nick's surfboard.

Nick lunged at him and grabbed it. "No way, dude." He stood with his back against the wall, holding his surfboard in front of him.

Tey whipped his knife out of the holster. Nick could picture what would come next: the sharp knife slicing his arm. Tey and the surfboard disappearing over the rails and heading across the river. There was a deadly silence.

Someone knocked at the door.

"Hi guys!" The friendly tour guide, dark curls blowing in the wind, popped her head inside.

Sheesh, Nick thought. Why the five-foot-something tour guide? Why not the six-foot-tall Rastafarian guy? Tey was a ticking time bomb. Nick had to defuse the situation before it got worse.

He thought hard. "Tey needs to get back to his village. Can the captain take the boat close to shore so he can swim in?"

The tour guide smiled. "Sure. Of course we'll help your friend." She glanced out toward the riverbank. "I see a village coming up now. Is that your village, Tey?"

Eyes brightening, Tey ran to the window. *"Si!"*

"Good! I'll let the captain know you want to go to shore."

Awkwardly, the three stood watching the little huts grow closer.

"Maybe Ronin Biri has your stuff," Madison suggested, anxiously studying Tey's tense face. "Is Ronin Biri your sister?"

Tey grunted.

"What was in the box?" Madison said, making bug eyes at Nick. "Was it really gold?"

"Yes. My gold."

"I didn't know it was yours."

Nick looked at Tey. "Why were the pirates trying to drown you?"

"They teach a lesson to my village—if you are a poor Indian, you work for nothing. Three dollars a day. You dig gold and hand it over. If you keep it you die."

Nick thought of the pirates pursuing him and Madison. He thought of the gunshots flying across the water. "Not good. Wasn't good for us either."

Tey cleared his throat. Then he rubbed his face with both hands. "I'm sorry, Nick."

Nick said nothing.

Tey said, "I'm sorry I told them you had the gold." He looked out toward the grass huts.

Nick nodded. "Okay."

Tey led a life so different than his. A dangerous, awful life. A life he'd never want to lead. Nick realized how lucky he was to grow up without the challenges and decisions Tey had to face every day.

What would Tey do now? He hoped Tey would find the gold.

I can't wait to get back to my surfing friends in Malibu, he thought. We fight over waves, but we don't try and kill each other.

Madison spoke up. "Tey. What does your name mean?"

Tey turned. For a moment, he was once again the cool, laid-back guy Nick had met on the cargo boat. Tey gave Madison an embarrassed grin. "My mama says it means hard, strong, and macho!"

Madison nodded, her face serious. "That's a good name."

She's become a peacemaker, Nick thought with an inner grin.

"Strong name!" Nick agreed. He figured Tey would need it.

He looked out at the broad, rushing river and the lush Amazon jungle. So peaceful-looking.

And yet so very deadly.

He could hardly believe how close his family had come to a horrible end. Thank heavens they were safe.

The tour boat engines stuttered to a halt and the Rastafarian crew member appeared. "Ready?" he asked Tey as they followed him out on deck.

"*Si.*" Tey started to climb the rails, about to dive down into the Amazon.

"No! No!" The crew member caught his arm. "We'll take the launch. Follow me."

"*Adios*, Nick," Tey said. "*Adios*, Madison."

"*Adios*," Nick said. "Good luck, Tey." He turned to Madison. "Come on, Maddy. Let's get a cheeseburger."

"And some yummy piranha?" Madison joked.

"After you!" Nick said, laughing.

His step-sis wasn't so bad—he might even teach her to surf when they got home to Malibu. She sure had the guts for it. Madison skipped ahead, but then ran back and grabbed his hand to make him hurry up.

"We did it, Maddy," he said. "You and me, little sis. We escaped the pirates!"

AMAZON GOLD MINING – 10 FAST FACTS

1. Gold mining has severely damaged southeast Peru
2. The price of gold is skyrocketing, drawing more miners
3. Miners must clearcut to dig up gold. Deforestation causes 30% of carbon dioxide emissions worldwide
4. In 1999, mines covered around 18,000 football fields. By 2009, that grew to more than 93,000
5. Gold miners dump mercury waste into rivers
6. Mercury poisons endangered animals and birds.
7. Local people eat the fish and are poisoned
8. Mining is done in 'low-governance' areas, meaning no police
9. Technology has mapped out thousands of new mines
10. Areas once covered with lush rainforest are barren, toxic wastelands.

WATCH

Mapping the Damage Caused by Gold Mining in the Amazon
By Carnegie Airborne Observatory ecologist Dr. Greg Asner
https://www.youtube.com/watch?v=SXeh5cqB30c

AMAZON PIRATES - 10 FAST FACTS

1. Violence in the region is rising, causing a sharp dip in tourism
2. With fewer tourist dollars, poverty-stricken locals may give pirates more young recruits
3. Attacks against oil tankers, cargo boats, and fisherman are becoming more frequent
4. Water gangs steal over $30 million a year from transport companies
5. Kidnappings have grown more frequent
6. Police boats rarely patrol crime-ridden areas
7. Pirates carry AR 15 assault rifles, machine guns, VHF radio, and high-powered binoculars. They're more heavily armed than police.
8. Drug cartels and other criminals fear pirates more than they fear the police.
9. One of the worst trouble spots is the upper Amazon near Iquitos. Another is the border between Peru, Colombia and Brazil
10. For locals, being attacked by 'water rats' is a constant threat

DOWNLOAD
This book's activity and
reading comprehension guide:
https://tinyurl.com/escaped-pirates

DID YOU KNOW?

Piracy has long been a fact of life on the Amazon River. Armed with sophisticated weapons and speedboats, pirates attack ships. They pillage cargoes, killing anyone who resists.

AMAZON RIVER PIRACY

In November 2017, pirates raided an Amazon river ferry. They stole jewelry, cell phones, laptops, cash, and even the ship's diesel fuel. A Californian family onboard hid in their cabin, but the family feared for their lives. At one in the morning, the parents and their two young daughters escaped into the river. They swam ashore using surfboards to keep afloat.

Afraid that local villagers were in league with the pirates, they hid in the jungle, home to jaguars, poisonous spiders, and anacondas. After four days, they saw a ferry boat and swam out to it, having survived a harrowing experience.

In 2001, pirates fatally shot New Zealand's world champion yachtsman, Sir Peter Blake. In 2017, British former school teacher Emma Kelty was robbed and murdered while kayaking the Amazon. Authorities suspect the so-called Water Pirates.

Recently, two clergymen survived being shot while preparing to teach a bible class. Pirates stole the belongings from 150 passengers on a riverboat traveling to Manaus. Others robbed 260 passengers on a cruise ship. And pirates took over a fuel ship and stole over 2,600 gallons of diesel fuel.

According to federal police, South American criminals consider pirates scarier than the cops. Pirates attack boats owned by drug cartels, illegal gold miners, and unlawful loggers. They kill the occupants, cut open their stomachs, toss them in the river as fish food, and claim the profits.

Violent attacks on local people keep riverside communities living in fear. Brazilian border cities like Manaus are among the world's most dangerous places. In remote, poverty-stricken villages, organized crime thrives. Residents complain that police boats rarely venture into these crime-ridden areas.

Villagers claim that there's no law on the Amazon River.

THE AMAZON RAINFOREST

The Amazon rainforest is called "the lungs of the planet" because its rich plant life stores carbon dioxide while releasing the oxygen we need to survive.

This immense rainforest stretches across eight South American countries. It covers a region nearly two-thirds the size of the entire United States.

The jungle is home to more than two million insect species, 100,000 plants, 2,000 species of fish, and 600 mammals, many of which are found nowhere else in the world. It contains huge reserves of gold, tin, copper, nickel, bauxite, manganese, and timber.

THE AMAZON RIVER

WIDTH: The Amazon is the world's widest river. Measuring 6.8 miles across in the dry season, it swells to a whopping 24.8 miles wide during the rainy season. The overflow dramatically floods its banks.

LENGTH: At 4,000 miles long, it's the world's second longest river.

SOURCE: It begins high in Peru's Andes Mountains.

Melting snow combines with tropical rainfall, sending it tumbling down the peaks and flowing northeastward across Brazil's low plains.

MOUTH: The Amazon River empties into a huge delta located in northeast Brazil at the Atlantic Ocean.

HOW THE AMAZON RIVER GOT ITS NAME

In 1541 a Spaniard, Francisco de Orellana, was the first European to navigate the entire Amazon River. He and his group were attacked by female Indian warriors and barely escaped. Orellana believed the women were descended from the Amazons, women warriors in Greek mythology. He named the river after them.

DESTRUCTION OF THE AMAZON RAINFOREST

Since the 1970s, miners and settlers have swarmed the Amazon, hungry for land and gold. Many scientists warn that development is harming the Amazon basin's fragile ecosystem, and that deforestation is contributing to global warming.

GOLD: In recent years, the price of gold has soared to $1,700 an ounce, causing an illegal gold rush in the area. Gold miners log and burn the forest, stripping away the surface of the earth to as much as 50 feet down. They use mercury to separate gold from grit, which poisons the rivers. Mercury seeps into soil, rivers and the food chain, poisoning fish and birds. It causes serious health problems in humans.

TREES: Thousands of illegal logging camps, both small and large, clear-cut valuable hardwoods using machetes, chain-saws, and heavy machinery.

FIRES: The rainforest is burning. Farmers have burned

and logged countless acres to grow crops and build roads for huge soybean farms and cattle ranches. Burn and slash methods for both legal and illegal crops have resulted in out-of-control deadly fires extending over thousands of acres.

DISEASE: The huge volume of immigrants have brought diseases like malaria, killing thousands of the Amazon's indigenous people.

INDIGENOUS PEOPLE: Many remain isolated from the world without medicine. As their homes and way of life are destroyed, their struggles grow as outsiders bring further violence and disease to the rainforest.

URGENCY: As of 2020, deforestation rates in parts of Brazil have doubled since last year. The future of the Amazon rainforest, a unique wilderness, is in jeopardy.

HELP PROTECT THE RAINFOREST

The Amazon is the largest remaining rainforest on our planet. Would you like to help save this incredibly precious place? Here are some things to consider:

- Only purchase responsibly sourced gold
- Read more books and articles to understand why the Amazon is important
- Create a habitat for migrating birds and insects, whether you have a balcony, windowsill, or backyard. It's fun and easy! Hang up a birdbath or a birdhouse, or plant insect attracting flowers.
- Buy recycled paper and toilet paper. Reduce paper usage. For example, use both sides of each of page. Exchange paper for cloth grocery bags, cloth napkins, and cloth cleanup towels. Eliminate paper

cups and plates. According to RainforestRelief.org, clearcutting for paper is one of the largest causes of rainforest destruction.

- Avoid palm oil. Read food package labels carefully.
- Avoid Amazon supplied beef. It can be difficult to know where food comes from, but try contacting suppliers, as well as voicing your concerns. Beef from clearcut ranches is often found in processed products and at some fast food hamburger chains.
- Avoid furniture, guitars, and items made from threatened Rainforest woods like Mahogany, Rosewood, Ebony, and all tropical hardwoods.
- Reduce your footprint! Drive a car with good gas mileage. Ride a bike. Walk to school or work. Start a carpool. Use public transportation. According to RainForest.org, gas companies have spilled over 20 billion gallons of toxic sludge and 17 million gallons of oil into Ecuador's rainforest and waterways.
- Support rainforest charities that help indigenous peoples and support conservation. *Rainforest Trust* buys land to protect it from deforestation and has saved more than 22 million acres of tropical habitat. *Rainforest Action Network* (RAN) convinced Burger King to stop buying beef from the Amazon. It convinced Home Depot to stop selling products made from old-growth rainforest wood.
- And remember, nothing is impossible. Good things begin with small but powerful steps. Take one today!

HELP PROTECT THE RAINFOREST

Give back, help the rainforest!
For every review we receive, we make a donation to Rainforest Trust.
Please give back by writing a short review!

About Rainforest Trust:

Founded in 1988, this group **buys land to save it from deforestation** and development and to preserve habitat. Its previous campaigns have included raising $100,000 to buy 1,992 acres of rainforest to help protect the Southern Woolly Spider Monkey. Celebrating 30 years of lasting conservation action, Rainforest Trust is proud to have saved more than 22 million acres of tropical habitat across 53 countries in 150 protected areas and wildlife reserves.

Study Guide
Download this book's activity and
reading comprehension guide:
https://tinyurl.com/escaped-pirates

Sources:

Ghinsberg Yossi, *Back From Tuichi*, New York: Random House 1993

Millard Candice, *The River of Doubt, Theodore Roosevelt's Darkest Journey*, New York: Doubleday, 2005

Angus Colin, Mulgrew Ian, *Amazon Extreme*, New York: Broadway Books, 2001

"Amazon River." Scholastic Grolier Online, go.scholastic.com/content/schgo/D/article/100/055/10005521.html. Accessed 15 Aug. 2019

https://www.smithsonianmag.com/travel/the-devastating-costs-of-the-amazon-gold-rush

https://www.nydailynews.com/news/world/family-back-u-s-escaping-brazil-pirates-surfboard-article-1.3621465

https://www.thehindu.com/news/international/pirates-of-the-amazon-rise-of-river-gangs/article20551450.ece

https://www.newyorker.com/magazine/2019/11/11/blood-gold-in-the-brazilian-rain-forest

https://www.adventure-life.com/amazon/articles/what-can-i-do-to-help-the-amazon-rainforest

THE I ESCAPED BOOKS

I Escaped North Korea!

I Escaped The California Camp Fire

I Escaped The World's Deadliest Shark Attack

I Escaped Amazon River Pirates

Coming soon

I Escaped The Donner Party

I Escaped The Salem Witch Trials

MORE BOOKS BY ELLIE CROWE

Kamehameha: The Boy Who Became a Warrior King

Nelson Mandela—The Boy Called Troublemaker

Surfer of the Century: The Life of Duke Kahanamoku

Wind Runner

MORE BOOKS BY SCOTT PETERS

Mystery of the Egyptian Scroll

Mystery of the Egyptian Amulet

Mystery of the Egyptian Temple

Mystery of the Egyptian Mummy

Join the *I Escaped Club* to hear about new releases at:

https://tinyurl.com/escaped-club

Printed in Great Britain
by Amazon

62359348R00076